MEG MEDINA

Milagros

Girl from Away

Christy Ottaviano Books

HENRY HOLT AND COMPANY

NEW YORK

Henry Holt and Company, LLC
Publishers since 1866
175 Fifth Avenue
New York, New York 10010
www.HenryHoltKids.com

Library of Congress Cataloging-in-Publication Data
Medina, Meg.
Milagros : girl from Away / Meg Medina.—1st ed.
p.   cm.
Summary: Twelve-year-old Milagros barely survives an invasion of her tiny
Caribbean island home and escapes with the help of mysterious sea creatures,
reunites briefly with her pirate-father, and learns about a mother's
love when cast ashore on another island.
ISBN-13: 978-0-8050-8230-2 / ISBN-10: 0-8050-8230-1
[1. Interpersonal relations—Fiction.   2. Mothers and daughters—Fiction.
3. Magic—Fiction.   4. Rays (Fishes)—Fiction.   5. Islands—Maine—Fiction.
6. West Indies—Fiction.   7. Maine—Fiction.]   I. Title.
PZ7.M512765Mil 2008   [Fic]—dc22   2007046939

First edition—2008
Printed in the United States of America on acid-free paper. ∞

1   3   5   7   9   10   8   6   4   2

*To those in my family who lost
their piece of paradise so long ago*

Milagros
Girl from Away

CHAPTER 1

Las Brisas

It's true that Las Brisas is not on any map, and for this reason there are always doubters, who say such a place never was. They're wrong. In fact, if you are determined, you can still find that old jewel in the Caribbean. You'll have to fly a tiny plane to get there, the kind with sputtering propellers and only two shotgun seats. And you'll have to fly it so close to the water that the cool spray will prick your skin. Only then will you see it—or at least what remains: a perfect circle of vegetation dotting the green waters, just a bump in the sea to an ordinary eye. Those who lived there peacefully are long gone, their bones and stories swallowed whole and cast about the world like broken shells. All that's left of it is the story of Milagros de la Torre, a brave girl, the only child known to have gotten out of Las Brisas alive.

In its day (which is to say, when Milagros was a girl of only twelve), Las Brisas had sand as white and smooth as flour. It was nothing like islands you might know in the watery neighborhood today—say, Grand Cayman, Cuba, or Jamaica. First, it was much smaller and infinitely more humble. You wouldn't have found fancy golf courses or foreign ladies holding frosty drinks decorated with tiny parasols. In fact, Las Brisas was so very small and remote that no big countries like England or Spain had ever bothered to bend it to their will. In all its history, not a single slave was brought to or taken from its shores. People simply didn't assign more value to some people over others, and as a happy result, no opportunists rose to bang their chests and start wars. And so, in the end, Las Brisas was just an innocent paradise untouched by modern ways, where people lived without any notion of being rare. It was this blindness to the world's darkness that blessed but later doomed that lovely pearl in the sea.

At the center of Las Brisas was a charming town that bustled with families and workers. The town gleamed with its wide, white streets and pastel buildings. It was squinty bright and hot at midday. But by four o'clock each afternoon, the air was cooled faithfully by a steady ocean breeze that fluttered ladies' skirts and filled the sleeves of men's shirts like balloons. Mothers scolded their children and chatted about the day's events over crooked picket fences. In the park, young ladies and heart-struck young men strolled along the green lawn.

Their hands only grazed as they walked by their shiny-haired fathers, who told loud jokes over dominoes and watched their children grow up out of the corner of their eyes. At night, children slept peacefully under mosquito netting. Each morning, still sitting in their beds, they drank sweet coffee milk from chipped porcelain cups.

This was the paradise where Milagros lived in a small house with her mother, not far from Avenida Central, a wide paved street that ran through the town's belly and ended at the glistening shore. Milagros walked the Avenida Central each day, passing all the stucco buildings—the post office, the library, the coffee shop, the lopsided fish shack—each painted the spectacular yellows, greens, and blues of a macaw's feathers. But it was the school that was especially beautiful in her view. Later she would recall how pleasing it was to cross its threshold. It was painted the orange and lavender of a sunset and had enormous floor-to-ceiling windows that let in the fresh air all day long. Three wide marble stairs ran across the length of the school and led up to the shiny wrought-iron doors. Through those doors you could see young Señorita Alma—her beauty and wisdom radiating from behind thick cat-eye glasses—molding them with patience. Together they studied the map; conversed easily in the musical sounds of at least four of the world's languages, depending on the hour of the day;

pounded out Mozart on the sticky-keyed piano; and breezed through addition drills with the ease of born mathematicians. It was Señorita Alma's laugh that one would hear in the school yard as she gathered her skirt sensibly around her legs and jumped rope like a child.

※ ※ ※

"¡Milagros, *bájate, por favor*! Come down from the tree and walk me to school," Señorita Alma said one morning, without even glancing up—mere seconds before Milagros had planned to pounce on her adored teacher. It was a daily habit, one that kept each of them alert in the mornings.

Laughing, Milagros landed on all fours in the dusty road, her books, bound with a thick book strap, in one hand. She was tall for her age, with crooked black braids and skin as white as a cup of cream. "How did you know this time? Did you hear me? Could you see me in the leaves?" she asked, dusting her knees off.

"*Ay*, Milagros," Señorita Alma replied without a trace of irritation in her voice. "I know all your tricks!"

"*Imposible*," said Milagros defiantly. She crossed her arms and added the protest in German, Portuguese, and English, too. "*Unmöglich! Impossível*—quite impossible!"

Señorita Alma tried to keep from smiling proudly.

She hesitated a moment. "Where is your *mamá* this morning?" she asked, peering through the kitchen window. "I was hoping to have a word with Rosa today."

"In the avocado rows," Milagros said simply. For good measure, she added, "She won't be home until sunset."

"I see," answered Señorita Alma, admiring the lovely roses that climbed the entire side of the small house. She leaned in and took a deep breath of fragrance. *The perfume of love,* she thought sentimentally. She would have to remember to ask Rosa the secret to such hardy specimens. The bloom Milagros had brought her last month had only just faded, long after it should have shriveled to seed.

"That one there will last long, too, *maestra*," Milagros said, pointing at a rose nearest the window.

Señorita Alma straightened in surprise and smiled. She clipped the large pink flower and started to stroll toward school. "Well, my little mind-reader, do you think I might talk to you, instead? Can you guess what I might want to say?"

Milagros's face darkened. She shrugged.

"Perhaps this will help?" Señorita Alma unzipped her satchel and reached inside. She curled her fingers around a palm-sized anole and held it out to Milagros. The black lizard inflated its red dewlap nervously.

"It seems someone put this lizard inside Eugenia's

schoolbag. She got quite a start. You know, the girl is given to fainting spells. It took Dr. López ten minutes to revive her."

Milagros took the lizard, stroked its head gently, and released it into the tall grass on the side of the road.

"Ten minutes? That's an awfully long time," Milagros said mischievously. "Is he a good doctor, *maestra*? Maybe he got distracted."

Everyone knew about the quiet romance brewing between the handsome doctor and Señorita Alma, a fact that made the older girls at school sigh with longing. Tall, with slick black hair and a wide, ready smile, Dr. López made all the girls titter when he peeked inside the schoolhouse each day to say *buenos días*. Even Milagros, who found most boys bossy and dull, looked forward to his daily visit.

Her teacher blushed and arched her brow. "That is beside the point, Milagros."

Milagros kicked at a pebble as she walked. She knew that it wasn't lovesickness or a lack of talent as a doctor that was the trouble. Like most adults, he had simply been duped. Why was it so hard for adults to see the truth of things? she wondered. Eugenia was the judge's sixteen-year-old daughter, a girl being raised to be as unobtrusive as a pretty knickknack on a mantel. The attention-getting fainting spells were a ruse. Milagros had once seen Eugenia practicing them behind her house. How conniving of that liar to faint into the arms of Dr. López, a man who belonged to Señorita Alma!

"Milagros, there is no need to scare the other children," her teacher continued gently. "It is not the way to have friendships. It only makes more trouble for you."

Milagros pretended to listen. It was useless to explain why these things had to be done. Señorita Alma was too kind to guess Eugenia's scheme. Still, Milagros hated to cause Señorita Alma pain. She thought guiltily now of what would happen later that morning. Perhaps she should mention the large tree frog buttoned inside the pocket of an art smock. Señorita Alma hated those noisy *ranas* and would not be amused. But it had also been Señorita Alma who had unwittingly given Milagros the idea in the first place.

"Detestable creatures," the teacher had muttered last week as she shooed the croaking green glob away with a broom. "Do you know, children, these tree frogs will cannibalize each other?"

If only you could see how perfect a remedy it is, Milagros thought now. A most suitable fate for Eugenia.

"You've made a mistake, Milagros," Eugenia had sneered in yesterday's art class. She was always torturing other people with a know-it-all tone that ate up everyone's self-confidence. "Your nose is much bigger in real life. You should draw some twigs and dirt in the hair, too." Giggles had floated from the other students at the back of the room.

Perhaps the frog will do the world a favor and eat Eugenia for breakfast. A cannibal deserves a cannibal, Milagros had thought as she buttoned the slimy creature inside the smock.

Señorita Alma's voice broke her concentration.

"Will today be a better day, then, Milagros? *Prométeme.* Promise me."

Milagros said nothing. As they rounded a mimosa tree, she froze momentarily and then pounced at the lowest bloom.

"Here you are, *señorita*," she said, opening her closed fist. An angry yellow hummingbird, no bigger than a bumblebee, darted away. Milagros raced after the tiny bird.

"Let's catch it again, *maestra*!"

Señorita Alma watched the lanky, barefoot girl go. *Talk is useless here,* she concluded. She knew better than to expect a day without a small disaster orchestrated by Milagros, anyway. She would have to find another way.

She broke into a run behind her favorite student, listening to the sound of trouble in the rhythm of their race. It followed Milagros everywhere. Whispers. Gossip. Humiliating family stories. All of these scraped and rattled behind Milagros, fastened miserably to her like noisy tin cans on a string.

CHAPTER 2

A Notorious Girl

Every family has its happy stories and its sad ones. The story of the de la Torre family was something more. It was a sad tale in a very small place, and so it was also notorious.

Milagros and Rosa lived in a modest house at the edge of the family's groves. Rosa was a farmer with almost magical skills. She was a quiet, serious woman, nothing like the other women in the village. She had inherited the land from her grandfather don Antonio, a weathered boat captain who had tired at last of his watery world after the sea swallowed up his only daughter and her husband. With just his beloved granddaughter, Rosa, for company he stumbled at last upon Las Brisas and ended his wayfaring days once and for all. Together, don Antonio and Rosa learned to love the land and the people of Las Brisas. Twenty rich acres of avocado trees made up their farm, and when don Antonio died, all of the land became Rosa's.

Rosa wore her wavy black hair short, and her palms, etched in dirt most of the time, looked like a dried map of roads leading this place or that. She was boyish, slim, and wiry, but her delicate face made her beautiful nonetheless. As often happens when someone is unusual, she had earned both careful respect and careless gossip among many women.

"She's odd," clucked Lourdes the butcher as she aimed her cleaver one morning. Twenty decapitated chickens lay in a pile on her counter. "Why, don't you remember when Milagros was born? She didn't so much as make a single blanket or ready a crib. She put Milagros in an empty avocado crate and set the child right alongside her as she worked." Lourdes crashed through the next bird, nicking her thick finger with the sharp blade.

Manuel, her husband, saw no problem with Rosa's arrangement. "For heaven's sake, the woman's a farmer. Where else would the girl be?" He handed his wife a white towel for the wound.

"Fine and good. But I'm a butcher, husband. You didn't see me sticking our María in the slaughterhouse, did you?"

Manuel laughed as he nudged Lourdes toward the

door. "Say what you will, woman. But it looks as though you'll need that crackpot, after all. She's the only one I know who can make a cut disappear into thin air. *¡Anda!* Go on, before you bleed to death!"

In the end, most of the villagers agreed with Lourdes: Rosa wasn't motherly, a fact that seemed unnatural. Even Milagros realized that Rosa did not keep the mental list most of the other mothers did: tooth brushings, clean clothes, and schoolwork to be reviewed. But was this bad? Milagros could never settle on the answer for herself. Still, she did not betray the slightest doubt to anyone else.

"You just get nagged and scolded for the slightest thing," Milagros pointed out righteously to classmates who might dare to ask why Milagros's blouse was wrinkled. "I, on the other hand, can run as I please. I come home long after dark, and nobody puts a switch to my legs or hollers in my face. I just come home when I'm tired, and that's perfectly fine. So don't bother me with your silly thoughts!"

But every so often, if she happened to overhear a mother calling for her children to come in for a bath, Milagros felt a tiny pang of shame. Why wasn't her mother worried about her? Why didn't she braid her hair or ask about her friends at school? Milagros never questioned her mother, though many times she would have liked to. Each time, as she got the nerve to speak her worries, something would happen to remind Milagros of the wondrous things that made Rosa a marvel. Rosa could be counted on in almost any situation. She was as sturdy as the ground that she tended. She could make a plant spring from even the sandiest fistful of earth. She cooked flowers and roots for their neighbors to cure colds, soft nails, bad luck, broken hearts. Why, only last year she had saved a toddler's finger when an angry sow had taken a deep, vicious bite. Not just any woman could do that, Milagros reasoned. "I'm glad Mamá is not like any other woman," she told herself. And for a time, this would quiet her private worries. Except for one.

Everyone knew—especially Milagros—that Rosa was not her biggest problem. No. That dubious honor went to her father, the unspeakable Miguel de la Torre. It was he who was at the very heart of the girl's troubles.

Miguel had abandoned his family to become a pirate. It was a shock to all who knew him, for Miguel de la Torre had been nothing more than a dreamy-eyed boy all his life. He liked to find horses and lions in the clouds rather than roll up his sleeves for a round of wrestling with ruf-fians. He admired his father's tales of adventure but was just as often found eavesdropping on the women telling love stories at their fences. He named turtles as though they were pets and not meat for soup. To no one's surprise, then, he grew into an utter catastrophe of a man who could not even wring a chicken's neck properly for a family meal. To his father's dismay, he had shown no proficiency in his studies, behind a plow, wielding a butcher's knife, or operating the post office. Miguel's only discernible skill was napping and daydreaming.

"That one is my greatest disappointment," his father had always complained at the fish shack. Oscar de la Torre was a burly man with no interest in anything beyond how high a price his lobsters would fetch at market. "What kind of man is he? He's good at nothing useful in the world! Why, his head is only good for holding up hats!"

When Miguel disappeared with pirates, the townspeople were speechless. "Miguel? A dangerous man? Preposterous!" they said.

But it was true.

It happened this way and with no warning at all. One night, an old-fashioned ship with bright red sails and a glistening ruby-studded mast arrived in the harbor. A scraggly sunburned captain stood in the crow's nest surveying the town.

"Who among you seeks to cut what binds you to

this island? I offer adventure on the seas! I offer you a world of riches and fame!"

The captain's blue eyes looked icy against his leathery skin as he scanned the faces turned in his direction. On the deck below, his crew of castoffs stood scowling before the crowd.

Slowly, the shocked people of Las Brisas inched out of their shops and homes. They surveyed the magnificent ship, wondering what was worth finding on a frightening monster like the ocean. Among them was Miguel, who had—of course—been napping beneath a shade tree, dreaming that the lives of other men were happier than his own. Rubbing the sleep from his eyes, he stood among his neighbors. Those who had laughed loudest at his expense and jeered at him for laziness had been reduced to trembling mice by a band of pirates. His father was huddled behind a stack of lobster pots.

Ah, he thought. *My answer at last.*

Miguel called Milagros down from the branches where she had been climbing perilously high. Only six, she squeezed between people's legs and bodies as her wide-eyed father jostled his way to the front of the crowd.

"Come, Papi," Milagros begged, pulling her father back. She was frightened to see her father hypnotized. She was even more frightened by the captain who held her father's gaze. He wore a single sparkling ruby earring that dangled the length of his dirty neck. The sight of him made Milagros want to hide herself and her beloved father.

But it was too late. Miguel was, indeed, under the spell of a man peddling a chance to be feared and remembered. He did not look at Milagros on the long walk home, hoping that in time they would forget each other completely. He walked in silence, making no comment at all, even when she did her best cartwheels to please him.

When morning came, Miguel was gone. All he left was a note for Milagros: *It will be up to you to make your way.*

"But why did he leave?" she demanded desperately, staring at the strange note, the last shred of a father who used to twirl her by the arms and tickle her until she was breathless. Rosa, silent in her own despair, let her face remain a stone as she held the wailing Milagros. How could she explain that doubt and ridicule had proven stronger than love?

So Milagros did all that was left to her that sad day. She tore up the note, locked up her father's face in her heart, and never mentioned him again. A terrible seed of sadness grew into a thick vine of distrust and disappointment. In time, it closed around her heart and left her with unruly ways.

And it was this stain, having the blood of a common criminal flowing through her veins, that kept every respectable girl away from Milagros's yard. Miguel had made Milagros a girl to be feared.

But even an ugly mark can have its benefit. And so it was for Milagros. She now lived outside of the games and carefree ways of other children, and she could see them all in a new way. To her surprise, it was impossible to hide a wicked thought from her. Cheating, lying, secretly insulting a classmate—she could see such schemes percolating quite plainly among the children. And without fail, Milagros quietly made sure the culprits paid a price for their cruelty. Pedro the cheater found that his plagiarized report had vanished. Carmen the insufferable gossip found her evil lies written word-for-word on the chalkboard. Andrés the gluttonous food thief found dead cockroaches in his stolen sandwiches.

"That girl is a serpent waiting to strike!" complained Eugenia's mother, yet again, to Señorita Alma. The tree frog hidden in the smock had tangled itself in Eugenia's hair before disappearing into her shirt. The whole incident had made all the children shriek and scramble on top of their desks. Her daughter was reduced to unseemly hysterics. "Rosa does not control her girl—it's hopeless." She lowered her voice to a conspiring whisper. "There is no strong man there to help guide that poor little disgrace! She will come to a bad end, I know it."

No amount of sensible talk by Señorita Alma had soothed the mother. And, sadly, it was true: Rosa, a woman oddly strong enough to run an entire farm, showed no ability to rein in a little girl. Instead, Rosa listened to Señorita Alma's report about her daughter that evening, her face inscrutable. It was the last of several complaints Rosa had been given that week:

"Your daughter tied a bell to my chicken's neck!"

"Your rascal dyed my daughter's ankle socks blue!"

"*My* child was missing her lunchtime pastry, madam. And *your* child had crumbs on her mouth! Will you explain that?"

Rosa offered neither apologies nor any promises to guide Milagros to a better path. She gave a gentle nod as the only sign she was even listening.

What no one knew, however, was that Rosa's silence did not mean she was numb to her daughter's suffering—or to theirs. Quite the contrary. Rosa was merely thinking in the way that farmers do. She knew bad vines coiled in the darkest parts of her groves. From one day to the next, they seemed to cover all in their path, finally choking the very trees they climbed. There was only one answer to a bad vine: Kill the roots.

It would be the same way with Milagros, Rosa concluded. How does one kill the roots of distrust? By learning to believe in the impossible, of course. It was time to share a secret, a marvelous secret that could cut loose the sadness tightened around her daughter's heart.

Milagros, still in her school uniform, lay in her hammock reading when Rosa appeared. It was nearly nightfall, and the air was filled with the sound of crickets and frogs. All the other respectable families were home eating their dinners together. Rosa, in her dusty pants and straw hat, was only now arriving from the fields. Milagros regarded her lazily. The creases around her mother's eyes were filled with dirt.

"The tree frogs are noisy this evening," Rosa observed. "They can cause quite a headache." Milagros did not answer.

"Come with me," Rosa said. She threw off her belt and the machete she used for clearing scrub. Then she reached for the leather pouch she always carried when she went exploring for new plants and cures.

"Where are we going, Mamá?" Milagros asked, swinging her legs over the side of the hammock. But Rosa did not reply.

Milagros cast her eyes down as they walked along Avenida Central, past the Carreras' home where all the underwear on the laundry lines had gone missing that very afternoon. She wondered, for an instant, if the complaint had yet reached Rosa. Or if anyone had noticed an old black goat wearing ruffled panties belonging to a girl who bragged incessantly about her fine clothing.

They walked until the street ended at the powdery sand and then made their way across the expanse toward the water. When she finally stopped, Rosa took a deep breath and stared out over the calm green water. The beach was abandoned.

"I learned this from my own grandfather. Don Antonio was a farmer, but also a man of the sea. He was a good man, Milagros, as many men are, though not all, as you and I both know," Rosa said quietly.

Without any further explanation, she had waded into the water and motioned for Milagros to follow. Milagros slowly came to her mother's side. Rosa closed her eyes, and Milagros waited. She felt foolish in a soaked school uniform that now clung uncomfortably.

She was about to complain—even defy Rosa as was

her recent habit—but then the water ahead began to shimmer in patches of orange, violet, blue, green, yellow. Each patch rippled beneath the surface like floating silk. Rosa kept her eyes closed and let a small smile slip across her face, but Milagros stood transfixed as the colors moved closer and closer.

It was a few minutes before Milagros could see that the floating mass of hues was a school of stingrays circling them. The rays were brilliantly colored, different not only in their flesh, but in their sizes, shapes, and varieties. Some were small enough to cradle in her arms, others longer than fishing boats. Milagros clutched her mother's hand and watched with wide eyes as one stingray's slippery body brushed her own legs. She was motionless, being careful not to step on the creatures' angry electric tails. Soon they surrounded Rosa and Milagros completely.

"Hello, little friend," said Rosa, petting the white belly of the smallest yellow stingray. She pulled from her pouch a tiny shrimp. She placed it in Milagros's open hand just under the surface. In a moment, Milagros felt the sudden suction of the stingray's mouth as it took the food eagerly. In appreciation, the stingray rolled sharply to one side and slapped its wing against the water.

"Those with the single spike on the tail, see? Those are bat rays," Rosa explained. "Careful of their wings."

Milagros pointed to two disk-shaped rays the color of blueberry pie filling. "Aren't these skates?" She had seen some of them at the fish shack. Not blue, of course, but the typical pale gray.

Rosa nodded, and she and Milagros busied themselves identifying, one by one, all the rays that had appeared. At last, Rosa broke into a smile. "¡Mira! Look."

She pointed toward a large patch of black so vast that it looked like a terrible hole had been opened in the ocean floor. But it was not a hole at all. It was a solitary ray, larger than any sea animal Milagros had ever seen. From fin to fin, it was easily the length of a house. Two great horns protruded from its face. It floated ominously, away from the others. Its size alone made Milagros feel afraid.

"Sailors call it the devil ray or manta—the biggest of all rays." Rosa tossed Milagros a shrimp. "He is harmless. Go see."

Milagros felt her heart racing as she waded slowly toward the creature that could easily overtake her. The closer she got, the larger and more menacing the creature seemed. Its eyes, she noticed, were fixed on her. Milagros stopped to look back at her mother, who was cradling an orange stingray.

"Go on."

Milagros turned back to the manta. She closed her trembling fingers around the shrimp. Her fist was much smaller than the manta's mouth, a mouth lined along the bottom with crooked teeth. She held her breath as she reached toward it. Its skin was shiny, like oil. She ran the fingers of her free hand tentatively along the manta's back, noticing that it felt like a wet mushroom. The mammoth fins, like huge wings, were solid, thick, and powerful.

Slowly, she lowered her palm into the water, and the manta ceased the gentle motion of its fins. Then it lunged with a single pulse and sucked up the shrimp with such force that Milagros fell back into the water. Sputtering, she scrambled to her feet to look at her hand. There was a tiny cut—a perfect circle—where the shrimp had been. By now, the manta had turned away and, with what looked like only two great thrusts of its fins, swooped out to deeper water where it turned again to watch from a distance.

Milagros was relieved to entertain herself for the rest of the early evening with several red bat rays. At last, when the sun dipped below the horizon and the rest of the shrimp were gone, the rays made their way toward the black manta. As Milagros and Rosa watched, they swam farther and farther, until, one by one, they all dropped to the sandy bottom, disappearing as mysteriously as they had arrived.

"How is this possible?" Milagros whispered to her mother as the two did a peaceful backstroke back to the sand. "Am I dreaming?"

"Not at all," answered her mother. "It's just a magic you hadn't allowed yourself to believe. There is much more of it in the world. You need only look where others do not see. It's everywhere around you."

Milagros and Rosa walked back down the Avenida Central hand in hand for the first time that Milagros could remember. Both were dripping, and Rosa's shoes squeaked with each step. The children of Las Brisas peered out of their windows to watch them make their way home. Milagros felt their stares, but to her surprise, she had no impulse to pull someone's hair or stick out her tongue. Instead, she felt the pride of someone who is trusted with a valued secret. She walked along thinking about the brilliant rays. For the first time since her father had left, Milagros felt happy to be unusual. Her distinction, at last, was for something other than being a girl left behind. Milagros closed her eyes and let this light reach the darkest corners where her sadness had been. Her mother, she knew, had given her a magical gift.

Of course, she could not have guessed then how priceless a gift it truly was.

CHAPTER 3

Market Day

Milagros took a deep breath and smiled.

Avenida Central was still damp with a few puddles where she could wiggle her toes. She loved the smell of market day: wet soil mixed with the soapy residue of newly cleaned sidewalks.

She glanced at the old man her mother was leading inside their market stall. It was amazing, Milagros thought, that *el viejo* José, a man of nearly ninety, managed to prepare the street for market each week. He was practically blind with milky cataracts in both eyes, and he sometimes forgot his own name. On at least two occasions, he had wandered into neighbors' beds, thinking they were his own. But José never failed to prepare Avenida Central for Saturday's market. As he had done every week since anyone could remember, the old man had scrubbed the street in a steady rhythm with a long-handled broom and a mountain of suds that smelled of pine. As always, he finished his task at dawn at Rosa's stall.

"*Que Dios te bendiga,*" he told Rosa in his thin, quivering voice. He made the sign of the cross with his raw hands. Rosa smiled at the blessing and guided him to the small cot she kept prepared for him at the back of the stall. She rubbed ointment into his swelled hands until they were shiny with oil, and then held the cup as he sipped her special tea. In no time, he fell into the peaceful slumber of men who live their purpose.

Rosa and Milagros began the last preparations for business as they did every Saturday. They had risen before dawn, hauling their fruit and multitudes of roses in their large, squeaky cart. Milagros arranged the fruit in a precarious pile on a table, ripest in front, as Rosa arranged her spectacular blooms in smaller containers. Milagros knew they would sell out completely. No one could resist Rosa's fruits or the flowers, she thought proudly. Perhaps, if the stall grew bare before the afternoon, she and her mother might have time for a swim at the beach. The rays might even appear. She glanced over her shoulder toward the sand at the end of the road. Two early-bird boys were tossing a baseball back and forth. *Shoo*, she thought. *Go someplace else.*

"You're keeping a secret," a man's voice said. Milagros jumped and turned to find Dr. López, Señorita Alma on his arm, at the stall. The sight of her teacher this way made Milagros feel awkward. Worse, as she looked past them, she spotted Eugenia, who stole furtive glances at the pair while pretending to examine cuts of beef nearby.

"Good morning, *maestra*," Milagros said, ignoring the handsome doctor. It was wrong to treat him coolly, but it was even more difficult to look at him and feel at ease. She had certainly kept him busy dispensing "calming pills" to patients who'd been victims of her pranks over the years. She was convinced he thought she was just a stupid child. As an alternative greeting, Milagros salted an avocado sample and extended the plate in the doctor's direction.

Rosa smiled and inclined her head politely. "*Buenos días*, señorita . . . doctor. You are here early today." She offered them each a velvety red rosebud.

Dr. López nodded. "Yes, enjoying the fresh air. It is good exercise, and you never know . . . maybe something exciting will happen at the market." He smiled mysteriously and glanced at Señorita Alma, whose cheeks burned pink.

Dr. López jerked his chin toward José. "Rosa, tell me: His old body can barely carry around his soul. How does he still manage to clean this whole street? You are doing something that science should know about. What is it?"

Rosa smiled serenely. She offered no answer, impervious to the doctor's charm.

Milagros pretended to busy herself stacking the fruit. She scowled at Eugenia, who was still gawking from across the street. Certainly Señorita Alma looked happy; any fool could see that. But Milagros couldn't help feeling a little jealous, not of her teacher, like Eugenia (now standing behind the sausages) and the other silly girls in her class. She felt jealous of Dr. López. Milagros simply liked it better when she had Señorita Alma to herself. What would happen if her teacher married this man and had children of her own? Milagros's heart darkened at the thought. Her teacher's love would have to run out. How could there be room left for a troublesome child like Milagros?

Señorita glanced at her watch at last. "*Amor*, the morning is getting away from us. Perhaps we should tell Rosa about the other matter we were discussing." Dr. López looked at his feet. "For me, please, *amor*," she coaxed.

He looked over his broad shoulder to see if anyone might be eavesdropping. Lourdes, the butcher, was safely doing battle with the bees and flies that plagued her beef stand. Eugenia had finally tired and moved on.

"Very well," he said reluctantly. "For you."

He looked timidly at Rosa. "It's nothing, but this lovely lady is a little concerned," he explained sheepishly. He rolled up the sleeve of his linen shirt. Large purple scabs covered his forearm, and each lesion oozed with infection. Milagros gasped.

"But you're the doctor!" she blurted out before she could stop herself. "You're supposed to fix things like this!"

"*Cállate*, Milagros. Be quiet," Rosa ordered.

"I was bitten by an insect a few weeks ago," Dr. López said, now fully red-faced. "This rash began as an itchy welt, nothing more." He lowered his voice to a whisper. "I've read all my manuals. I've tried the usual antiseptic and even antibiotic. It should have healed by now—"

Señorita Alma interrupted quietly. "Rosa, he is having fevers at night. It may be serious. And, in any case, you understand how tongues wag." She inclined her head at Lourdes in the nearby stall. "It will be bad for Amado as he sets up his practice. They will say what Milagros has already pointed out. 'Look, the doctor who cannot even cure himself!' Will you help us?"

"I cannot cure what people say. No one can," Rosa said quietly as she examined the doctor's lesions more closely. "Milagros, bring me my pouch."

Milagros stepped over José, who was now snoring loudly. She grabbed Rosa's large leather pouch. The bottles inside jangled like little bells.

Rosa rummaged through her sack and extracted a bag of brown leaves and a blue bottle, the contents of which she combined in a mug and stirred with her finger. Finally, she poured the mixture into a clean rag and signaled the doctor to come closer.

Dr. López looked apprehensively at Señorita Alma. She drew herself closer to Milagros to block the view of outsiders.

"It looks as though the doctor has something to learn, eh, Milagros?" he said. Milagros felt her cheeks flush as he spoke her name. She hadn't meant to be impertinent.

Rosa wrapped his arm in the rag and buttoned the sleeve back over the compress. Before Dr. López could thank her, a loud voice boomed through the stall and startled them all.

"There you are, López!"

It was the mayor, looking flustered in his white suit. The man knew only one tone of voice—that of a circus ringleader.

Señorita Alma smiled sweetly and parted the way. "*Sí, alcalde.* He is right here."

"I've been looking everywhere for you!" He motioned his hand impatiently. "It's almost time. Hurry, now! Both of you!"

"It's almost time for what?" Milagros asked Señorita Alma as her teacher and the doctor hurried after the mayor.

"It's a surprise, *mi hija*," she answered. "I know you love surprises. We will talk about it later." She looked at Rosa and whispered, "*Mil gracias*, Rosa. A thousand thank-yous."

"*¡Bienvenidos, señores!*" The mayor's voice echoed off the white steps of the government offices. He beamed over the people gathered below as he waited for quiet. A student of theater once, he loved the power of a dramatic pause before opening the weekly market. They had all grown used to his antics by now. Early shoppers waited patiently, straw baskets in hand, as they turned to face the mayor. A respectful hush fell over the crowd.

The mayor glanced at a sheet of paper where he had jotted down the opening announcements. "Señora Cruz announces that she has new fabrics imported from Spain this week, excellent for skirts and dresses. She can offer help with patterns, as well. Héctor Suárez tells us he has had a good haul of shrimp this week. Thank you, Suárez! *Enchilado de camarones* is my favorite dish, so I hope some of you will invite me for dinner, hmm?" He waited for the chuckles to die down.

"For those who might have forgotten your mail yesterday, Marietta will be available under the yellow umbrella if you wish to pick up your letters. Is there nothing else? No?" He pretended to study his list and then slapped his forehead dramatically. "Oh, of course, there is one more announcement. How could I forget?"

A murmur went through the crowd as Dr. López and Señorita Alma climbed the steps to join the mayor. The doctor slid his arm around Señorita Alma's waist. Milagros felt her stomach lurch.

"I bring you all wonderful news today. The moment we have long been waiting for has arrived. Las Brisas will soon be celebrating a wedding! It is my pleasure to announce the engagement of our lovely Señorita Alma and our esteemed Dr. Amado López!"

The crowd erupted into cheers and applause. Milagros watched mutely as men slapped Dr. López on the back, and Señorita Alma disappeared inside a circle of excited women all talking at once. Several schoolgirls in the crowd huddled around Eugenia, who went pale and, for once, truly lost consciousness.

Rosa turned away from the happy spectacle and

returned the bottles and leaves to her pouch. She spoke over her shoulder to Milagros.

"It is not what you are thinking," she said. "Love is not cut up into little rations that are used up. When there are full hearts, there is always more to share. That is how it will be with those two."

"What do you know about love, Mamá?" Milagros muttered to herself.

Rosa seemed not to have heard. Instead, to settle the matter, she turned and shoved an ugly white root into Milagros's hand. She motioned her head toward Lourdes.

"Take this to the butcher. Tell her this will end her problem with flies."

Later that evening, Milagros sat on the sand and watched Dr. López as he marveled at his cured arm. His scabs had disappeared without a trace even before the market had closed, and now he and Rosa were conferring seriously beneath a palm tree. Several of Rosa's herbs and bottles were spread out before them on the sand.

Señorita Alma sat next to Milagros, who buried her own feet absently. The four had enjoyed a private picnic dinner on the beach during which Milagros had fought the urge to be gloomy. Everyone loved Dr. López, after all. He was a fine man. She had no right to be selfish about her teacher.

Señorita Alma nudged her softly. "What is it? Aren't you happy for me, Milagros? You do not want me to marry this man?"

Milagros tried to smile over her loss. "It's not that," she said. "He is good enough. Well, maybe not as a skin doctor, though," she added petulantly.

Señorita Alma threw her head back and laughed. "Amado will find that very funny."

"Please don't tell him," Milagros said urgently. "He'll really hate me then."

Señorita Alma looked surprised. "Well, I doubt very much that he would hate you. You are absolutely one of his favorite girls. He tells me that clever mischief is a sure sign of great intelligence. He is always defending you."

Milagros studied Señorita Alma's face for a lie. "Really?"

"Certainly." Señorita Alma put her arm around Milagros. "I notice a big change in you lately, Milagros. You're getting older and wiser. I would consider myself very lucky to have a daughter just like you someday."

Milagros's heart sank. *That is precisely the problem*, she thought.

"There is only one you, of course," Señorita Alma continued. "But perhaps as a wedding present, you would be willing to do us a favor?"

"A favor, *maestra*?"

"Of course! As you can see, Amado and I both have a lot to learn about everything. But mostly, I want to know how to raise a smart, strong girl. The best way to do that is to study the subject as closely as possible. I hope when we get married, you will stay with us whenever you like. Think of it this way: It will be your turn to be the teacher."

Milagros gazed out into the water and considered the offer. "Only if I can tell Eugenia about our arrangement," she said, grinning.

Señorita Alma laughed. "Very well." She stood up and stretched. "I'm going in for a dip." She handed Milagros her glasses. "Would you like to come along?"

Milagros watched her teacher stroke powerfully out to deep water. Then she glanced back at Rosa and the eager young doctor. The day had brought a little magic after all.

CHAPTER 4

A Secret Discovery

The terrible trouble began as imperceptibly as a wave lapping on the shore.

One winter evening, after she had finished playing with the rays, Milagros spied something bobbing at the water's edge. It was a lovely red bottle, the ruby color of red wine, and it was streaked with salt and sand. Around its neck, the glass was raised in the shape of many starfish, each touching the next like a chain. The bottle was tightly corked, but Milagros could see a sheet of paper inside rolled to the thickness of an ordinary pencil. She sat on the sand and began to work the black cork carefully with her molars. After a few moments, she shook the open bottle into her palm and freed the tiny scroll.

Happiness and jealousy are bad cousins. Beware, the curled paper read.

Milagros pondered the words but could make no sense of them.

She ran home at once to share her discovery with Rosa, who was at the stove. Little crescents of dough bubbled in hot oil as Rosa poked at them with a long fork.

"Have you been down at the beach?" Rosa asked without looking up when Milagros entered.

"Yes, and—"

But she did not finish her words. She had a secret, a small mystery of her own. She slid the bottle inside the waistband of her shorts instead.

"And?" Rosa asked.

"And . . . the water had a bit of sea lice today," she said.

Years later, Milagros would replay that conversation in the kitchen, her lost opportunity to tell someone about the message in a bottle. She would wonder sadly whether telling Rosa at that moment would have saved her beloved Las Brisas.

But, of course, she did not tell. And some mistakes, however we wish to undo them, simply cannot be undone.

※ ※ ※

Here is what Milagros did instead.

She hid the bottle beneath her lumpy mattress and

lay awake imagining its most exciting origin. In the afternoons, when Rosa was gathering fruit, she took it out to let the sunlight shine through it. Sometimes, she walked the beach until dark searching for more clues. She found none.

"You seem awfully interested in that book," Señorita Alma noted one afternoon as she addressed her wedding invitations. Milagros sat at her own desk with her nose buried in a dusty volume called *Cuentos del mar*. She had asked for quiet reading time after school to examine the books she had dug out of her mother's trunk. They had belonged to don Antonio, Milagros's great-grandfather, and they were all about life on the sea. The moldy smell of the pages was making Milagros's nose drip.

She looked up, sniffling. "Did you know it was once a crime in England to uncork a bottle in case the messages had come from spies?" she asked. "Queen Elizabeth made it a capital crime."

Señorita Alma took off her thick glasses and wiped them on the bottom of her skirt. She was delighted by Milagros's sharp mind.

"Really? I did read once about a message that was found a hundred and fifty years too late. It was sent by a man on a sinking ship. Can you imagine it, Milagros? Writing as one's vessel sinks into frigid waters? Falling into the jaws of some sea monster and still having the presence of mind to send one last message into the world! It's all so . . . incredible, isn't it?"

Every nerve in Milagros's body tingled. "What did the message say?" she asked.

"Nothing romantic, I'm afraid," Señorita Alma answered wistfully. She liked romantic stories, especially now that her wedding was approaching. "It was simply the name of the ship and its fate. Nothing more."

"Well, what about sea monsters, then?" Milagros asked, closing the book and edging her way to Señorita Alma's desk. "You said he fell into the jaws of a sea monster."

"Hmm? Oh—no, probably not. It's just an expression. You've heard the tales. All you have to do is stand around the fish shack with the old-timers; you're bound to hear something. Sea serpents, sharks. Or huge devil rays that will suffocate you in their wings and drag you to the bottom of the sea. My mother told me that one plenty of times."

"Well, it's not true," Milagros said quite firmly.

Señorita replaced her glasses and smiled quizzically at her student. "It's just an old wives' tale, Milagros, all of that nonsense about sea monsters. It's late now. Let's leave that book for another day."

"They don't kill people," Milagros said again. "Mantas don't kill people at all."

"Very well, then. I am corrected. They don't," Señorita Alma said, giving up. "Help me shut the windows, please. We are expecting rain."

☀ ☀ ☀

"Do mantas kill people?" Milagros asked Rosa at dinner that evening. The mere thought of being wrapped in a manta's body had made her nervous all afternoon.

Rosa placed a platter of fried plantains on the table and laughed. "No, never on purpose. A sting here and there, perhaps."

"Señorita Alma's mother told her they did. That they drag their victims out to sea and drown them."

"Milagros, people say many things," Rosa said, sitting down. "You must learn to see and know with your own eyes and mind. Adults will tell stories to make children mind rules. What better way to keep a little girl from deep water than to tell her she will be stolen and drowned?"

Yes, Milagros thought to herself as she took the first bite of her dinner. *Adults can be liars.*

CHAPTER 5

The Rubians

The bottle stayed beneath Milagros's mattress, her thoughts of sea monsters and dying seafarers suspended as a new excitement grew. For now it was February, carnival time, and the people of Las Brisas were in preparation.

Carnival time was the happiest time of all. For three days the whole island would leave behind its mundane routines and erupt into a party of food, music, and dancing. With its stores and offices closed, all of Las Brisas would gather on Avenida Central. Restaurants would serve food in tents outdoors. The mayor would sing loud love songs from his youth. Mothers and fathers would dance on the streets long into the night, forgetting even the names of their own children.

But the best part was the evening parade. Hundreds of performers from Rubia, an even tinier island to the south, would arrive, bringing with them music, magic, and spectacle. There were bottle jugglers, drummers with their bodies painted white, fire eaters who smelled of ash, women whose eyelids glittered with sequins, stilt walkers strolling majestically like giants from another world.

It was because of the parade that Milagros had happily volunteered to remain after school. Dr. López sat nearby, stuffed behind a student desk, cutting strips of crepe paper with a pair of surgical scissors. Milagros snipped the last sheet of hot-pink crepe paper into quarter-inch squares of confetti. She had managed to fill three large bags for Señorita Alma. Now her neck hurt, and she was nursing a blister. Still, she didn't complain. The children always climbed to the school's roof and rained down the brilliant confetti on the procession of plumed dancers below. Milagros loved to watch the tiny flakes flutter in the air, pieces sticking here and there to the revelers' hair or to their shiny skin.

Milagros looked at her swollen finger and then at the clock. It was almost dark.

"Do you think this is enough, *señorita*?" she asked, rising.

The teacher was bent over, stuffing the last of twenty homemade piñatas with candy. She straightened, stretched her back, and regarded the lopsided parrot piñata she held in her hand. Her hair had fallen out of its pinned bun.

"Quite! There simply is never enough time to prepare, is there? Thank goodness I have you as a helper. Oh, and you, too, of course, *mi amor*," she said.

"I'm sure it's easier to do surgery than to mince all this confetti," Dr. López joked. He rolled his cramped shoulders and stretched his spine. "It's getting late, isn't it? What time are you supposed to be home, young lady?"

Señorita Alma glanced out the window and clapped her hands. "*¡Ay, mi madre!* Time's gotten away from us, Milagros! I've kept you too long. Hurry home before it gets darker. Dr. López can walk you there. My apologies to Rosa, please. *¡Gracias!*"

A loud clatter made them both jump. Dr. López had caught his long legs under the desk and toppled backward. Milagros peered over the upended desk. "Don't bother getting up, doctor," she told him as he lay flat on his back. "I'll make it home in a few minutes. *¡Hasta mañana!*"

Milagros hesitated for a moment on the school steps. With the shops closed, Avenida Central was deserted. She took one step toward the street, but reconsidered. If she crossed the beach, she would be home faster. She headed toward the ocean in the growing darkness.

As Milagros reached the sand, she slowed to take in a most curious sight approaching in the water. A large shape, like a dark iceberg, loomed at the shore. As she squinted, she could see that the shape was actually a collection of small rowboats and rafts floating toward shore, all of them sagging and in disrepair. There were people aboard. Large boxes of cargo were perched awkwardly one on top of the other. Milagros slid behind the trunk of a palm tree and watched.

Several men jumped into the water and began to tie the rafts and boats together. Women slid into the water, hitching small children to their hips or balancing large baskets on their heads before moving toward the sand. They worked in silence until all the cargo was unloaded. The people looked frail, like dark skeletons. They were hungry-eyed, and their hair was uncombed. Most of the men were shirtless. They walked silently in a single file away from Avenida Central to the north side of the island, where there was nothing except mosquitoes and snakes.

Milagros stepped out from behind the tree as two men hitched an enormous box to a third man's back. She watched the line of people disappearing into the darkness. She thought for a moment of walking back to the schoolhouse and asking Señorita Alma about the strangers. Surely they were not the Rubians, not this somber group. But if not Rubians, who were they?

Milagros took a deep breath and decided to get a better look at the collection of boats and rafts they had left behind. The rafts bumped gently in the lapping water. There were no markings and no special equipment except for ropes, small buoys, and heavy stones that served as anchors.

She could not make out any detail in the darkness. She would have to come take a look at things in the morning. She turned toward home.

But Milagros was not alone. Standing close enough to touch was the most beautiful boy she had ever seen. He was taller than Milagros, thin and muscular, and he wore his shoulder-length hair loose. His large, dark eyes held her gaze steadily. An unsmiling young woman stood next to him. She wore the impassive expression of a lion considering a pounce. She narrowed her eyes as she stared at Milagros. Her face was thin and her cheeks hollow.

Milagros could feel an unspoken menace. It was far worse than the secret mischief of children. This was an icy evil reaching to her throat.

"I—I was just looking at the boats," Milagros stammered as her mouth went dry. "I was just curious."

The boy let a slow smile creep across his full lips, an act that made Milagros shiver. The lion-faced woman kept her indifferent gaze on Milagros. Then she bent down and picked up two long pieces of wood. Draping them across her skeletal shoulders, she turned and headed toward the others.

"Come, Delfín," she commanded.

By the fourth step, she and the boy were cloaked completely in darkness.

CHAPTER 6

The Rubian Delfín

Rosa was not home when Milagros arrived, and the house seemed unnaturally quiet. Milagros locked the doors for the first time she could remember and waited for her mother. She knew Rosa, unfortunately, would be late. Her mother had warned her that she and her men would work into the night to make up for the carnival holiday. At midnight, Milagros, sleepy and waiting, lay on Rosa's bed and closed her eyes.

In the morning when she awoke, she was still dressed but tucked beneath the covers. A pair of dirty work pants was piled on the floor. A note rested on the night table. *I will meet you at the parade. Be in front of the butcher shop. Eight o'clock.*

Milagros lay back on her mother's pillow and closed her eyes in frustration. She had slept fitfully during the night, and now she'd have to wait even longer to get answers about the strange arrivals. Rosa would be working deep in the groves by now; it would be nearly impossible to find her. Besides, her mother would not likely welcome an interruption for a silly question about Rubians.

Milagros turned over in bed, her mind once again on the gaunt strangers from the beach. Their faces had chased her all night long into the darkest corners of her dreams. Even now, in the safety of her mother's bed, their memory chilled her. She studied the clock and made a decision at last. She slid on sturdy work boots that could stand up to the prickly bushes of the island's north quarter and headed for the door.

* * *

It took the better part of an hour to reach the strangers' camp, which was hidden deep in the brush. She followed their trail of trampled grass and twigs carefully. As Milagros made her way farther into the north forest, the morning light dimmed beneath the thick canopy of trees until she found herself walking in near darkness. She had been here only once with Rosa to search for wild herbs. Milagros paused to rest by the large boulder she remembered as a landmark, realizing that this was as far as she and Rosa had come. The familiar patch of delicate, purple flowers spread down the slope to the left, but Milagros felt no urge to pick them or roll in their fragrance. Instead, she studied the ground ahead for any sign of a footpath. Peering into the darkness, she noticed a narrow opening in the thorn bushes and decided to follow it.

She listened carefully for the sounds of animals that might be watching her approach: rodents, lizards, and snakes, any of which might attack if disturbed. She stepped as lightly as her boots would allow, keeping a careful eye on the shadowy ground. A sobering truth now occurred to her: A poisonous bite in the isolated north forest would be fatal. She had left no note regarding her whereabouts; it would be hours before anyone would even notice she was gone.

She shook her head to banish her frightful worries. *Think of something else*, she told herself firmly as she side-stepped a prickly vine. *Something interesting.*

Delfín came to mind instantly.

Milagros thought of his long gaze and startling smile. She had never seen a boy like that in Las Brisas, worlds away from the weak sort whose mothers fussed over them endlessly and who were easily disarmed with a prank. Delfín's expression had been unflinching and daring—an unspoken challenge.

She climbed the first of two steep hills. Reaching the

apex, she heard voices. She crossed a clearing and edged her way up the second hill, grabbing thick tree roots to help her over the top ridge. Moments later, she knew she had discovered the camp.

Milagros crouched behind a rotting stump and looked around carefully. The camp must have been used as their base each year, for it was located around a clearing where the rest of the thicket was almost impenetrable. It would be impossible to clear such scrub in a single night's time.

The strangers had arranged stones in a large circle, and several charred logs remained smoldering at the center. The faint smell of cooked fish hung in the air. Feathered carnival headdresses, costumes, and drums were strewn all about the campsite. Recognizing the lavish Rubian costumes at once, Milagros began to feel foolish. She had seen the Rubians late in the night, when any traveler would be tired and irritable. Under those conditions, of course they would seem unfriendly. She had been silly to be frightened of entertainers. What explanation would she offer now if discovered? She leaned back against the stump to think.

A breeze rustled the treetops, and a tiny glint of light on the ground caught Milagros's eye. There, beside a small tent, she spied a stack of machetes and knives. The collection of so much glistening weaponry gave her pause. Surely these were meant for clearing a path through the thicket. But wouldn't two or three such knives be sufficient to chop vines and brush for the group? She made a silent count of the knives. There were enough to arm dozens.

A murmur of voices emanating from the surrounding tents interrupted her thoughts. She tucked back deeper into her hiding spot, straining to make out the words in between the spurts of rough laughter. Unfortunately, the Rubian dialect was tricky despite all the languages she had studied with Señorita Alma.

As the voices grew louder, Milagros began to wish she were invisible. Plain young girls with dusty, thin bodies gathered in pairs to prepare their makeup for the night's performance. With each layer of rouge, lipstick, and glitter, the small, hungry girls vanished. Their lips were painted burgundy, and their eyelashes now curled to touch their arched eyebrows. One by one, their false visages in place, the garish showgirls made their way back inside their tents.

Milagros scanned the area carefully when, at last, no one remained in the clearing. She strained to see a large sheet of paper that she had not noticed before. It lay near the knives, held down at each corner with a stone.

Milagros crept closer and saw that it was a large, hand-drawn map. She flattened herself to the ground and inched forward, determined to inspect it thoroughly.

It was a map of Las Brisas. All of the island was marked clearly. The bank, the post office, the various shops—they were identified in sloppy lettering. Milagros was surprised to see that even her own little house and the groves were drawn and labeled. The mayor's house and the government building were circled repeatedly in black and starred.

She let her mind race over all the possible explanations. The dread she had felt so clearly on the beach had returned; her hands began to perspire.

Her instincts made a quick decision simple. She would show this map to Rosa. Surely her mother would want to know about knives and a suspicious map. Milagros made her way closer, still on her belly, and then darted out to the open space. In a flash, she snatched the map and tore back toward the brush.

She sped down the first hill, a thorny branch ripping painfully at her thigh. Reaching the bottom, she stopped to check her wound. It was not deep, but the gash was wide beneath her torn pants. She pressed her open skin together and waited for the bleeding to slow.

Then she heard a small snap.

Milagros straightened slowly and turned to face back up the hill. No one was there. She strained her eyes to see into the dark bushes; still nothing. Casting a furtive glance over her shoulder, she considered the only familiar way out. She would have to cross the small clearing and descend the second hill.

One hand still clamped over her cut, the other clutching the map, Milagros backed slowly across the flat expanse toward the trees at the edge of the precipice. At last, her foot caught the thick roots she had used earlier to scale the top of the hill. Without looking, she knew the long, rocky incline fell away sharply behind her. She let out her breath and turned to make her escape.

The hill was dangerously steep, but Milagros rushed down as fast as her clumsy boots would allow. She nearly stumbled several times, but fear urged her on through the thicket. She leaped over roots and fallen trees, determined to reach home.

But now a new sound met her ears. Close behind her, footsteps were crashing through bushes in her direction. She leaned forward to gain speed, but it was no use. The runner was closing in on her with each stride. Finally, a hard shove sent her tumbling to the ground, her cheeks scraping painfully as she rolled down the hill. She cried out and grabbed frantically for anything that might slow her. With a sudden, rib-crushing jolt, she was pinned facedown by someone's foot. Milagros looked over her shoulder in fright and gasped.

There stood Delfín.

"Let me up!" she demanded.

He held his foot firmly between her shoulder blades.

"I said, let me up!" she said again.

Delfín pressed harder for a moment and then took a step back with an amused expression. Milagros struggled to her feet and stumbled away from him. She picked up the map and wiped her bloody cheek nervously, aware that he was studying her. The new cut stung badly, but she refused to cry in front of him, a satisfaction she never gave bullies. Instead, she pretended to ignore the fact that he was staring.

"You should stop spying on us," he said at last.

The sound of his deep voice surprised her. It was not the unpredictable squeak of bossy boys at school. Milagros picked a sharp stone embedded in her cheek and flicked it in his direction. She tried to glare, but quickly looked away. She saw immediately that Delfín was older than she was and even more handsome in the daylight. It made her self-conscious to look at him. His eyes were light brown, the color of his caramel skin, and his silky black hair hung loosely around his broad shoulders. She, on the other hand, was a bloody mess.

"I'm not spying," she lied.

He raised his eyebrows. "No?" He jutted his chin toward the stolen map in her hand. "What's that, then?"

Milagros's face blazed, and her eyes brimmed with tears. "You tell me. I think *you* are the ones spying," she shot back. She shook the map in his direction. "You've drawn where everything is on Las Brisas."

Delfín considered his options for a moment, and then he took several steps toward her. Milagros gripped the map and fought to stare back at him defiantly as she braced for his attack. Instead, he reached toward her face gently to remove a twig caught in her hair.

"You are pretty in the daylight, too," he said matter-of-factly.

Milagros grew furious. He was mocking her the way boys always did when they wanted to show they were stronger, or, worse, he was treating her like a baby.

"So are you," she snapped. She wanted her words to shoot out, perhaps even imply that he was girlish with his loose hair.

Delfín folded his arms across his bare chest and regarded her for a few moments. "Why are you here?"

She cleared her throat nervously. "I came for a walk."

"A walk? Way on this side of the island?" He flashed a bright smile and drew his machete from his belt. He picked absently at the ground with its tip. "That's a lie."

Milagros felt her tongue go dry. Her eyes darted to the path that led down the remaining hill and back to his worrisome knife.

"You look frightened," he said darkly.

"Not at all," Milagros insisted. "I don't frighten easily." She edged her way closer to the path. "It's just that I need to get back home before the carnival. My family will be wondering where I am."

Delfín smiled wickedly. "Will they?" He looked up at the forest canopy for the sun. "Then you should go. It's almost time for the carnival. You won't want to miss all the fun we have planned for you."

Nothing in his voice sounded lighthearted or joyous. Milagros eyed the long blade in the mottled sun once again. She took a deep breath and turned toward the path.

In a flash, Delfín leaped out and grabbed her arm. He bared his teeth, and his hot breath filled her face.

"The map stays here," he hissed.

Milagros tried to pull away her hand, but she found herself clamped in Delfín's iron grasp. She was surprised to hear her own voice. It was as though another girl were giving form to the last of her sensible thoughts. "Why have the Rubians drawn a map of my island, Delfín?" she whispered.

Delfín leaned into her ear like a little boy with a delicious secret. Milagros shuddered.

"Everyone needs to know where they're going," he said. He slid the map easily from her limp hand. "Go on now, pretty girl. Your dear family is waiting."

He released Milagros quickly, turned his back, and strode powerfully toward the Rubians' camp.

All she could remember of him as she raced for home was the sparkle of his weapon, the white of his smile. Evil and beauty joined in a wicked world.

CHAPTER 7

Viva Las Brisas

Milagros returned home almost at dark. In the distance, she could hear drummers and trumpeters practicing and horns honking. She took a long shower, hoping to clean out her scrapes and scratches and to erase her encounter with Delfín. She hurried into clean clothes.

Everyone was buzzing with happiness. People had already begun to place empty beach chairs on either side of Avenida Central to secure the best view for the night's parade. By the time Milagros had begun to snake her way through the crowds toward the butcher shop, every inch of the street was filled with giddy revelers. She scanned the crowd for a glimpse of Delfín as she made her way toward the music.

The air felt full of electricity as people clapped and swayed to their favorite samba. A wooden stage had been erected near the post office, and the first of many bands was performing. Sweat streaked down the cheeks of the trombone players. Musicians on the cowbells shuffled their feet and kept the beat. A conga line was forming in the crowd. The chief of police, shaking maracas and wearing a lady's hat, was in the lead.

"Stay out of trouble tonight, you little rascal," he called to Milagros merrily.

Milagros laughed out loud. She bought a coconut candy and sank her teeth into the sugary lump as she watched a young boy try his luck with the piñata stick. He barely made a dent. She pressed on through the crowd, worried that she would miss Rosa. The parade was about to begin, and then she would have to cross to the school in time for the confetti drop.

She had just not yet reached the meeting spot when a high trumpet note sounded, the note that signaled the start of the parade.

"*¡Señores!*" cried the mayor. Dressed in a white suit, he stood on the platform stage holding a microphone. "I welcome you all to the very best carnival in the very best island in the world. *¡Viva Las Brisas! ¡Viva Las Brisas! ¡Viva Las Brisas!*"

An enormous cheer went up through the crowd, and everyone jostled forward. Milagros felt herself being propelled by the horde. She dropped to her knees and scurried between people's legs to the curb, where she would have the best view.

Up ahead, the first glorious dancer appeared to lead the procession. She was a tall, light-skinned woman in an enormous feathered headdress that glittered with shiny blue stones. Like the other dancers behind her, she wore a small brassiere made of delicate cowry shells. Her muscular stomach was exposed above a white skirt edged in bright ruffles. Her ankles and wrists were ringed with dozens of gold bracelets.

She sauntered barefoot as hoots and whistles filled the air, and she held her arms out wide to display her costume for all to admire. Her full lips were painted red, and her smile was constant, almost unreal. Her eyebrows arched dramatically as she moved her head carefully from side to side to greet the cheering crowd. When she was a few feet from Milagros, she stopped. She fixed her eyes on Milagros, and the entire procession froze. An expectant silence filled the street. Then she curled back her lips and let out a loud, high-pitched wail, a musical sound that did not seem quite human. And then, with a single bang of the drums in unison, the very last carnival in Las Brisas began.

Down the street they came, the dancers swaying their hips and arching their backs until their heads brushed the ground behind them. Men, naked to the waist, did breathtaking flips while holding machetes that they clapped loudly in the faces of the onlookers, who jumped back nervously. Drummers let out piercing shrieks as their beat became faster. A dozen dancers hidden behind large carved masks spun to keep time with their feet. The procession seemed to last forever, each moment more exciting than the one before. All the while, Milagros searched the performers' faces for Delfín.

At last, Milagros could see her favorite performers at the end of the street: The stilt walkers were approaching. A huge roar erupted from the crowd.

They moved like creatures in an underwater dream, slowly lifting their legs and placing them carefully. They towered over the parade, their wooden legs making them taller than most buildings on the street. Bright silk scarves attached to their legs and arms billowed in the breeze.

Looking up, Milagros suddenly realized she had lost track of time. She was late getting to the rooftop of the school. Already she could see Señorita Alma handing out bags of confetti. If she didn't hurry, she would miss the confetti drop. There was no time to cross at the end of the street. The only solution was to sprint across the parade's path before the stilt walkers reached her.

Scrambling out behind the machete dancers,

Milagros reached the middle of the street when, unexpectedly, the machete dancers turned to face her. They moved into a circle and slapped their sharp weapons together to ensnare her. Their smiles seemed pasted in place. Confused, Milagros felt captured, but her fear faded as quickly as it had risen. The machete dancers opened their circle as quickly as they had closed it. They turned and continued on.

But now it was too late for Milagros to cross. The stilt walkers were upon her.

"Get out of there, Milagros," she heard a familiar voice call. It was Dr. López, looking worried, on the other side of the street. But soon all she could see were the bright scarves of the Rubian stilt walkers. She tried to cross, but each time she moved, a huge orange, pink, or green leg seemed to block her path. She looked up but could not see their faces.

Suddenly, two of the stilt walkers bent over. In a moment, Milagros was hoisted up by her arms and legs until she was held high, flat on her back. The stilt walkers passed her from one to the other as the crowd cheered. Milagros laughed once, but as the game continued, they tossed her roughly in the air and caught her too tightly by the arms. Milagros could feel her stomach lurch, and her arms ached.

"Put me down," she yelled. But the music drowned out her shouts. She was finally passed to a yellow stilt walker.

Milagros stiffened. There, behind the yellow face paint and the wide, false smile, was the lion-faced woman she had seen with Delfín at the beach the night before. Her eyes gleamed wickedly once again. She tossed Milagros high in the air. This time, no arms came out to catch her, and she plunged downward. She was only inches from the ground when the machete dancers caught her, to the delight of the crowd.

"Good-bye, pretty spy," she heard Delfín's voice say, though she could not tell from behind which of the masks his voice had come.

The lion-faced woman bent low toward Milagros. "Enjoy yourself, girl. While you can," she said. Then she lifted her body in a slow swoop and was gone.

The parade continued toward the beach, where food and drink awaited them all. Milagros felt a chill run down her spine as she watched the crowds trail happily. She did not follow. Confetti fluttered in the air as the music began to fade. She sat down alone on the school steps, stunned and silent, picking pieces of the festive paper from her hair. It was Dr. López who rushed to her side.

CHAPTER 8

Secrets Revealed

Milagros lay in the hammock, thinking. She wasn't afraid, not exactly. Still, she had absolutely refused to return to the carnival, and now, on the last day was counting the hours until the Rubians would sail their ramshackle boats back to their island. *Good riddance,* thought Milagros. Delfín had not shown himself during the carnival. How foolish to have wanted to see him! The Rubians—especially Delfín— were not to be trusted. Why was she the only one to see it now?

"Don't be silly," Señorita Alma had said when Milagros mumbled that there was something wrong with the Rubians. "You had quite a scare, that's all. These are the same people who've helped us celebrate carnival for years and years." Señorita Alma and Rosa had been thrilled, at first, to see Milagros as part of the parade.

Milagros watched Rosa at work in the kitchen. With no workers to help in the field, her mother was at home.

Swinging her legs over the side of the hammock, she walked to the house. She put her face inside the open window and took a deep sniff. Rosa was at the stove, stirring a large pot of cornmeal for lunch. Milagros said nothing for several minutes.

"Tell me about Rubia," Milagros said at last.

Rosa looked up. "The Rubians again," she said with a sigh, shaking her head slightly. "They have made an impression on you."

"They have a terrible look in their eyes, Mamá. Don't you believe me?"

Rosa turned down the flame and walked to the window. She looked at her daughter patiently.

"If that is what you see, then I believe you."

"Then please tell me what you know about them," Milagros insisted.

Her mother returned to the stove and dipped the tip of her ladle into the pot. She blew carefully and offered a taste to Milagros through the window.

"To be honest, Milagros, I don't know very much. We are close neighbors in the world, but far away in how we live."

"What do you mean?" Milagros asked.

"Think of our own Las Brisas. Our soil gives us enough to eat. The ocean is clean. We help one another in hard times. We have enough work to help us feel useful. But that is not the way everywhere. Rubia is one such unfortunate place. Poor little Rubia is nothing but a rock in the ocean. It will not yield a single grain of rice to feed its people."

Milagros thought of the hollow cheeks of the lion-faced stilt walker. She thought of the ugliness in the eyes and the bitterness that had laced Delfín's deep voice. It was not hatred, Milagros realized. It was jealousy.

Milagros's stomach tightened. *Happiness and jealousy are bad cousins*, she thought.

Beware. Then she thought once again of the Rubians' map.

"Beware," she said aloud.

"Beware? Beware of what?" Rosa asked.

"Wait here," she told her mother, and she disappeared from the kitchen window. Returning breathless, she slid the bottle across the kitchen table and watched her mother carefully. "I found this."

For a moment, Rosa did not move. She was transfixed by the bottle. Finally, Rosa picked it up almost reluctantly and shook out the scroll. She ran her fingers over the handwriting, held the paper to her nose and breathed deeply. Then she held the red bottle up to the light, turning it to study its neck.

"How long have you had this?" Rosa asked finally.

Milagros shrugged guiltily. "A couple of weeks, maybe."

Rosa pressed her lips into a thin line of disapproval. It was the same look she had worn the morning Miguel had vanished from their lives forever.

Milagros gulped down her shame and continued. "I've seen them, Mamá. I've watched them. They mean us harm."

"Who means us harm?"

"The Rubians. I went to the north side to spy on them. They have a map of our whole town. Even our groves are marked." She could not bring herself to mention Delfín.

Rosa turned off the flame beneath the pot and headed toward the back door at a quick pace. Milagros stared after her.

"¡*Oye!* Where are you going with my bottle? It's mine—I found it, remember?" she called.

"Stay here, Milagros," Rosa said firmly, pulling off her apron and tossing it onto a chair.

The screen door banged behind her.

It was many hours later—long after the sounds of the carnival had begun—that Rosa came home. Milagros had made the unhappy choice of eating five pastries and drinking a glass of milk for her dinner. Now, besides feeling angry and worried, she had a queasy stomach. She had just begun to doze in her bed when she heard Rosa tiptoe in and place the red bottle on her nightstand.

"Where have you been?" Milagros demanded in the dark.

Rosa jumped. "You frightened me."

"Where did you go with my bottle?" Milagros pushed up to her elbows. "It's *my* bottle. You shouldn't just take it without permission," she complained. "And you should say where you are going. I ate alone! Should a girl be left to eat alone, too?" Milagros reached over and grabbed the bottle for safekeeping. She knew her words were ugly, but she could not bring herself to show relief at having her mother home.

"Yes, it's yours," Rosa said, sitting on the corner of the bed.

"So, where were you?"

"Trying to learn a bit more about this little find," she said tiredly.

"Where do you think it came from?" asked Milagros.

"A friend. Of sorts," she said absently.

"Who? Who would warn us?"

Rosa looked at the bottle in her daughter's hands

and said, "I'm not sure. I spoke a few words with Señorita Alma and Dr. López, but they have noticed nothing unusual. I tried the mayor, but he was busy singing to his wife. The chief of police was not to be found, either, though I waited an eternity," she said wearily. "It's hard to speak with anyone at carnival time, of course."

"But why do you have to talk to anyone at all about it?"

Rosa sighed. "Because I think you are right, Milagros. This message is a warning. Our little island may be in danger. They need to know, to be prepared, if it's not too late."

Milagros felt her face flush.

"It's about the Rubians, isn't it?" Milagros said.

Rosa stood up, becoming lost in the shadows of the room. She was silent for a few long moments as if deciding what to say.

"Well?"

Rosa was at the doorway now. "We have not worried about anything outside our beautiful place, Milagros. We have made it easy for envy to root and work against us." Rosa gave a heavy sigh. "It could be the Rubians. It could be many, many others. But this is too much talk for a hot night, isn't it? And I'm tired. Go to sleep now. Carnival is over tonight, and nothing out of the ordinary has happened. Perhaps nothing bad is in store. This could be a silly hoax, after all. In a few days, when things are back to their usual way, we can think more about this note."

Before Milagros could argue, she heard her mother glide out of the room. She turned to the wall and closed her eyes, the bottle cradled like a tiny baby beside her. She felt both angry and, now, a little afraid.

Are we truly in danger? She pulled her knees up to her stomach to ease the cramping.

She went to sleep that night dreaming of the jackal smile on Delfín's face.

CHAPTER 9

Attacked

In the days following the carnival, Las Brisas became dreadfully still and hot. The temperature was creeping up, and thick nimbus clouds the color of a shark's skin filled the sky. Even at midday that Tuesday, it seemed as though night was upon them.

The children had at least thirty minutes until they could go home to eat lunch and enjoy their hammocks. They felt thick-headed and sleepy, thanks to the late nights of the carnival. The gentle clicking of the wooden chimes in the hot breeze left them all in a stupor.

Only Milagros seemed to feel restless despite the heat. She was halfheartedly reciting her multiplication tables with the other students, scanning their sleepy faces to see what the trouble might be. The twelves were so easy, even in English—the language of choice for their morning studies. She could chant the answers and still watch people, especially Señorita Alma, who was across the room. She cleaned her glasses repeatedly. For the first time Milagros could remember, she had turned the lock on the wrought-iron door. Every few minutes, she pulled on the bars gently, as if to make sure the lock had engaged.

Señorita Alma wasn't even listening. She seemed distracted today. Milagros wondered if it had to do with the wedding, only a week away. But Milagros was not convinced. The teacher had stopped by Milagros's house that morning and had whispered to Rosa in the doorway. *More whispering,* Milagros thought bitterly. She had drawn pictures in the dirt with a stick as she waited for Señorita Alma and her mother to finish.

Everywhere the adults seemed to be whispering—at the fish market, over dominoes that no one seemed to be playing in earnest. When the children entered a room, the adults were struck silent or else they began talking loudly about nonsense.

"The weather is hotter than last year, eh, Juan? Very hot."

"My, but that's a tasty banana I'm munching. María, have you ever tasted such a sweet banana?"

The whole thing infuriated Milagros, who was not used to being treated like a girl with glass ears. Whatever it was, Milagros was sure it had to do with the mysterious note in her bottle (now safely hidden under her mattress once again). Rosa, who had finally met with the mayor, offered no further explanation when Milagros asked.

But Señorita Alma could not hide from her scrutiny. She stood now near the iron gates of the front door peering down the street every so often, as if expecting a visitor. She had not smiled this morning at all, and she had nearly jumped to the ceiling when Pedro Santos dropped his math book on the floor.

"*Doce por dos, venticuatro,*" the class recited. "Twelve times two, twenty-four."

"That's very nice. That's fine," she said to the class, still staring through the bars, as she interrupted them. She fixed her eyes down the Avenida Central toward the ocean and squinted. A look of relief seemed to flood her face. Moments later, Dr. López was at the locked gate. The two whispered an exchange.

"Little friends, today we will not play our game in the courtyard," Señorita Alma began, turning quickly from the door. The children were so surprised, they didn't even groan. Milagros sat up in her chair.

"I'd like you to go to your homes for lunch, and we will leave a little early today. We will go now. Girls, please line up here; boys, by the windows, please."

Milagros hesitated. What was wrong? She pushed in her chair and, being the tallest, stood at the end of the line by the door.

Señorita Alma unlocked the gates and stepped out into the daylight, blinking. Dr. López took her gently by the arm. She shielded her eyes and looked up and down the street.

"All right," she said almost in a whisper. "I want you to listen carefully and do exactly as I say. Go home quietly. Take the fastest way possible. Do you understand?"

Thunder began to rumble, but there was no rain yet. Señorita Alma pulled back the iron gates, put a finger to her lips, and silently signaled the shocked children to go. The children spilled down the stairs like ants swarming from a mound. Their feet made tiny clicks on the steps as they descended.

When Milagros was about to go through the door, Señorita Alma grabbed her hand. Milagros could feel a jab of fear run up her own arm.

"We will go with you, Milagros," Señorita Alma whispered.

"What are you doing here, doctor?" Milagros asked.

"Quickly, please," Dr. López said, ignoring her question. Señorita Alma locked the gate as quietly as she could. She put an arm around Milagros's shoulder, and the three made their way toward the road. With a glance back toward the sea, Dr. López quickened his pace. "Hurry!" he said.

"*Señorita*, what's wrong?" Milagros asked, rushing to

keep up. "I'm not going another inch until you tell me!" Milagros stopped, out of breath and resolute.

There was a long roll of thunder, and Milagros looked up at the threatening sky. In an instant, she knew the sound was not coming from above. Señorita Alma was already staring past her in horror. When she turned to look down Avenida Central, Milagros was dumbstruck.

The street behind them was filled with masked men on horseback, the animals' hooves lifting a low cloud of dust. Covered by a haze, the advancing men were like ghosts in a terrible dream. In the lead came a man who waved a burning club and bore a sinister grin. He let out a shrill cry. The men broke their stampede formation and raced toward the terrified people, who tried desperately to barricade themselves inside houses and storefronts. The attackers smashed store windows, grabbed kicking children by their waists, and set buildings ablaze. The tiny fish shack, where so many townspeople met to chat over coffee and crackers, ignited like paper. Women screamed in the streets and burst from doors and windows as the marauders broke into their homes and emerged clutching valuables.

Milagros watched all of this as if in a dream. Her feet were rooted to the ground. Then she felt herself shaken suddenly.

Señorita Alma screamed. "¡*Ay, Dios mío!* Run, Milagros!"

Two attackers broke away from the melee and charged toward them. Milagros was jolted into action and raced for her life, Señorita Alma and Dr. López several paces behind her.

Milagros dodged down the deserted side street lined with areca palms that led to the far end of her mother's groves. She could see the safety of the dark avenues of trees up ahead. If she could only reach the groves.

"This way," she called blindly.

The smell of ash began to burn her nose. Milagros could hear the rhythm of a horse's hooves coming closer, and soon she could feel the hot snorts and breaths of the animal over her shoulder. From the corner of her eye, she spied the rider's red scarf covering his nose and mouth. He leaned down toward the horse's neck, fixing his eyes on Milagros, and reached for her with a bejeweled hand.

Milagros dodged madly, taking an enormous leap inside the first row of avocado trees. She made a hard right, running between the trees so that the horse could not easily follow. Deeper and deeper she ran into the shade of the trees. Señorita Alma's scream pierced the air. Gunshots rang out.

Milagros raced until her lungs ached and her sides

felt as though they would explode. It was several minutes before she realized that the sound of the horse's
hooves had stopped. The only sounds now were her
labored breath and the river that ran alongside the
groves. She crouched at the base of a tree to think.

What is happening?

She was far inside the rows and down too low to see.
She glanced upward at the tops of the avocado trees. Her
mother had often warned her of the brittle branches,
especially on the older trees. Taking a deep breath, Milagros grabbed the lowest branch and flipped herself up
like a circus performer. She scurried as high as she
dared, hidden by the foliage, until she found the crook
of two branches.

Milagros let her eyes roam the floor of the grove
below. The sight froze her in terror. Dr. López lay on his
side in a pool of dark blood. Curled at his chest lay
Señorita Alma, her eyes wide and blank. A gust of wind
swayed the branch, and Milagros gripped it tightly,
fighting the urge to swoon.

She leaned back carefully into the branches and
squeezed shut her eyes. "Oh, God in heaven, don't aban-
don me now," she begged silently. Suddenly a rough
hand covered her mouth.

"Don't scream," a voice said.

CHAPTER 10

Escape

Rosa climbed down from the upper branch like a cat, one hand still clamped over her daughter's mouth. For the first time, Rosa's face seemed to have lost its inscrutable calm. She looked frightened as she regarded her daughter. Her eyes were red and watery.

"We must get you to the ocean," she whispered fiercely. "I have no time to explain. I will take you if I can. If we are separated, Milagros, please be obedient this once. Get to the shore. You will find a dinghy waiting for you."

"*¿Qué dices?* A boat? Why would I need a boat? Where am I going?"

Rosa froze for a moment and pointed to her own ear, signaling for Milagros to listen.

Voices were coming very close.

"Not so lucky now, are they?" sneered the tall man on the left as he exhaled a long stream of cigarette smoke.

"We make our own luck," said his younger companion with a laugh.

Peering through the leaves, Milagros saw two thin men approaching. They wore no shirts, and their hats were down low over their foreheads. Rubians. They walked almost casually, slicing low fruit from the lowest limbs and stuffing it into sacks as they went. The younger man paused, removed his hat, and fanned himself.

Milagros gasped. It was Delfín.

He paused at the sound, his hand on his machete exactly as Milagros remembered. He let his alert eyes scan the trees. Milagros and Rosa remained motionless.

"*Vamos.* They're here somewhere," said the taller man. Delfín seemed to be staring directly at Milagros. He narrowed his eyes and hurled an avocado as far as he could. The whizzing fruit grazed the leaves near Milagros's face before smashing into the trunk of the next tree. It sent a spray of light green mush in all directions. Rosa leaned back into the leaves and held her breath as another gust of wind swept through the groves. Black storm clouds began to roll slowly, and the tree vibrated with the rumble of thunder.

Milagros gripped her branch tightly as the wind picked up. She could hear the old wood of the tree creaking. Delfín and his companion were almost directly under them now. One more gust of wind rushed through the leaves, and without warning, Milagros's branch gave way with a sickening snap. She lurched for Rosa's hand, but it did no good. Together they crashed through the skinny branches and landed in a heap on the ground.

For a moment, no one moved. The shocked Rubians were like two statues, mouths open, providing just enough time for Rosa and Milagros to burst into a run. They raced to where the farmland ended and gave way to open sand. The ocean waters behind the house were churning gray and white in the wind.

"*¡Corre*, Milagros! Run! Do not wait for me," Rosa shouted as the tall Rubian reached and grabbed her arm roughly. His eyes flashed, piercing Milagros, freezing her in terror. "Get to the ocean, Milagros!" screamed Rosa. "Go now! You will know what to do."

Milagros ran across the sand, not daring to look back at the smoking island or at her mother's fate. She could hear Delfín panting behind her.

Sand pricked her thighs like broken glass as she ran. Ahead she could see a dinghy bobbing in the water. It was just as Rosa had said. She trudged against the turbulent waters and then dived beneath a crashing wave to get some distance between her and her pursuer. She swam underwater until her lungs ached and then came up for a gulp of air. She kicked and reached as best she could, but the boat seemed no closer. The waves crashed into her face and rolled her under again and again until she could no longer breathe. Below the waves, she opened her eyes and saw only silt and shells and had no idea which direction was up. Kicking her legs, she managed to break the water's surface.

"Help!" she screamed. But the only reply was the sloshing of water and the rumble of the sky. Her heart pounded. "Mamá!" she cried one last time. A huge swell crested in front of her, and next she felt the enormous crash of water hitting her like a board on the head and shoulders. This time, she was sucked straight to the sandy bottom. Her face and arms were scraped by jagged rocks.

Milagros could see only blackness. Unable to draw a breath, her heart thundered in her chest. She knew she would not reach the top. *I will die here and now,* she thought desperately. She opened her mouth for air, and a rush of water filled her lungs.

But it was then as her chest seemed to compress that Milagros heard her mother's voice. *You will know what to do.*

Milagros willed herself to stop fighting. She stilled her arms and let the water toss her. Her thoughts grew calm at Rosa's words. Her chest eased.

As she slipped into the quiet place between life and a watery death, she found that it was not frightening anymore. It was as if sweet breath were being blown into her lungs. Soft, slippery blankets seemed to wrap her, making a safe bundle that the raging waves could not disturb. The water stopped crashing. Instead she swayed like a baby in a hammock, her thoughts traveling over the green hills of Las Brisas, through the marketplace noisy with bargaining men, along the hard dirt road leading to her home. She could see all of Las Brisas at once. In no time at all, her limp legs thumped against the wood of the small boat that had seemed so far away. Without any effort of her own, her back and arms were lifted over the side and she gently rolled in.

Rest, now, Milagros, she could hear the large stingray tell her as real air filled her lungs again.

But where will we take her? another voice asked.

Milagros sputtered saltwater and felt her world go black. The dinghy moved farther out into the ocean. It was the last she would ever see of Las Brisas.

CHAPTER 11

The Ruby Pirate

Milagros lay for days in a sleepy stupor as the rays gently bumped and nudged the dinghy deeper into the sea. When she finally awoke, her empty stomach growled. Her hair was matted and salty, and the skin across her nose and cheeks was covered with painful blisters. She squinted into the blue sky and pushed herself up on her elbows. Her tongue felt fat inside her mouth. Where was she?

"Rays?" she croaked. She listened, but there was no response. She stared hard into the water, but she could make out no shimmering colors. Milagros sat up straighter and shook her head. Lifting her eyes, she gasped.

Anchored before her was an enormous ship, its red sails bound tightly near the crow's nest, where a single gull sat pensively. The masts were inlaid with rubies the size of a child's fist. She recognized the ship immediately. It was the ancient ship that had crowded so many of her dreams. It was the very ship that had lured her father away.

The deck appeared abandoned. She held on to either side of the wobbly dinghy as she focused her eyes on the sparkling sight. There was a pattern carved along the length of the vessel that she could not make out in the bright light. Milagros glanced around for the oars and quietly used them to make her way closer.

It was a red glass band that trimmed the entire ship. Dancing inside was a pattern of starfish, the same pattern that had decorated her prized bottle.

Milagros was transfixed as she made her way around the ship to a gangplank that reached out over the water. At the very edge stood a tall man with copper skin and black hair drawn into a long, thin plait. He wore only crimson trousers that fluttered in the wind. His back was to her.

"I see you have grown," he said coolly as he turned to face the dinghy.

Milagros froze. She knew the voice and the gentle eyes, even if his hair had grown long and his skin had browned. Staring down at her from the gangplank was her father, Miguel de la Torre.

For years she had dreamed of Miguel returning home, scooping her up, and explaining that he had been kidnapped, that no father would have abandoned her in favor of selfish adventures as all the townspeople whispered. And yet he was here in good health aboard a pirate ship. Anger grew into a lump in her throat.

She stuck her oars awkwardly into the water and began to row away frantically from the ship—to where, she did not know. Weak and confused, she managed to travel only a few feet before moving in frustrating circles.

"And where do you think you will go now, Milagros?" Miguel chortled. He straddled down on the gangplank, his legs dangling over either side as he watched his daughter struggle to row.

"I don't care where I go! Far from you is all I want! I don't care if I drown in this ocean!" shouted Milagros.

Miguel's eyes flinched at her words.

"I see," he replied. He looked up at the sky, thinking. Finally, he looked down on her again. "Well, go if you must. But I am surprised at your haste. Aren't you curious about your own father? About what I can finally offer you after all these years? A cup of water at the very least?"

Milagros hesitated.

"Come on, Milagros. The others are gone; there's no danger. It's just the two of us on the *Ruby Sails*." He leaned forward and steadied his body along the length of the gangplank. He stretched out his arm. All his fingers were ringed in gold, though his nails were chewed to the nervous stubs of a liar.

"I can't trust you," she said finally.

Miguel gave a wistful grin. "True. But what other choice do you have?" His soft eyes held her gaze.

She turned her face and considered her situation. She wouldn't last long without freshwater and some food.

She heard a splash and looked up. Miguel had vanished from the gangplank. Suddenly, his head popped up near the dinghy. His dark eyes flashed, and a devious smile spread from ear to ear.

"Here," he said, rolling in easily. "Allow me to escort you, daughter." Milagros dropped the oars and turned her back. The seagull watching from the crow's nest took flight. A long, mournful caw filled the air.

The first hour in the ship's cabin was quiet except for the slurps and gulps of Milagros filling her mouth with fruits and salted fish. She seemed barely to notice Miguel, who watched carefully.

"Greasy little lips and hands," he mused quietly. "You used to sit in my lap to eat fried chicken."

Milagros stopped eating and looked up, startled. She remembered those times exactly. The smell of her father's linen shirt. How he let her wipe her sticky hands on his trousers without concern for how his friends might laugh at his lax discipline.

"I don't remember that," she said, trying to be cruel.

Miguel's eyes darkened, and he sobered his tone immediately.

"Yes," he said sadly. "It was the life of a different man, wasn't it?" He stood and focused his eyes instead on his glittering rings until Milagros was through.

"Better now?" he asked when she pushed away her plate. Receiving no response, he fished in his trouser pocket and pulled out a small, rusted tin that he slid across the table. "Your face is in tatters. Take this."

Milagros examined the tin but couldn't make out the drawing that had been corroded by the salt air. She twisted open the lid and instantly recognized the familiar mint smell. It was the green ointment Rosa often made from aloe and mint leaves, a sure remedy for skinned knees and burns. Tears welled up in her eyes. What she wouldn't give at this moment to have Rosa's calm presence nearby. Milagros quickly rubbed the salve on her blisters. She shivered as the tingling ointment soaked into her swollen skin. Then a terrible thought seized her. She stared defiantly at Miguel.

"Where did you get this?"

"It's not important," Miguel answered.

"I demand to know what's happened to my mother and to *everyone* on Las Brisas, for that matter."

"Demand?" Miguel threw back his head and laughed. "First of all, I don't think you're in a position to demand much of anything, Milagros. And secondly, I'd say you've become rather impertinent since we last saw each other. Is this how you should talk to your father?"

Milagros snapped the tin shut and shoved it into her pocket. The word *father* stunned her for a moment. "When we last saw each other, sir, you decided that having an adventure was more important than taking care of me," she said quietly. "I don't see the smallest reason to be kind to you."

Miguel stood from the table and walked slowly toward Milagros. The brass handle of a knife glinted at his side as she eyed him warily. Following her eyes, he loosened his belt and laid the knife far away on the floor. Unarmed, he sat on the corner of the table near her chair.

"Kind? Do you think I still wait for people to be

kind?" He looked closely into Milagros's face, studying the turn of her lips, the angle of her nose. Both were his stamp on her.

Milagros noticed his scrutiny and set her jaw. She hated being alone in this dark place with Miguel. She hated hearing the same voice that had once called her from below the treetops where she had liked to hide.

"You are uncomfortable, Milagros?" he continued. "Are you afraid the father who left you behind is a devil, eh? Perhaps you're right. Maybe there is no forgiveness for the choice I made. But there is no turning back, is there? I am a pirate now." He leaned in still closer. "But I wonder: What about you?"

"Me?" Milagros asked. "What are you implying?"

"You like excitement, too, little girl. Don't pretend you don't. You've had adventure in your heart since you came wailing into the world. I remember your laugh. Why, it barreled through the house when you did something mischievous." Miguel stroked his daughter's hair. "It was a pirate's laugh."

Milagros shrugged off the touch of his fingers.

"It was nothing of the kind," she shot back. "Pirates hurt others. They steal. They kill. I'll never want to do any of those terrible things. There's nothing to be proud of in that."

A pained look passed over Miguel's face, and in a moment, his eyes flashed.

"So, this is your choice? You, too, will curse the name Miguel de la Torre?"

Milagros did not reply at once. She ran her fingers along Rosa's tin in her pocket, gathering her resolve.

"I'd like to know about my mother—and about what hand you played in all this mess," she whispered finally.

Anger clouded Miguel's face. He crossed his arms and stuck out his chin. "Why would I know anything?" he snarled.

"I'm not blind or stupid. This design on your ship: It's the same as the message bottle you sent to Las Brisas. You've done something despicable, and I want to know what it is."

Miguel blinked for a moment as though startled. He straightened himself and smiled.

"Very well. You think me despicable, and despicable I will be. *Despicable* is a pirate's favorite word, in fact." He patted Milagros on the cheek, though it was almost a little slap. "I have absolutely no idea what's happened to Rosa. She could very well be dead. There's nothing I can do about it."

"Dead?" Milagros repeated. Her throat constricted as she remembered the huddled corpses of Dr. López and Señorita Alma. She ran her finger over the tin in her pocket once more and shuddered.

"This may all be for the best," Miguel said, turning from her. He rose and climbed the narrow steps leading up to the deck. He looked back at his once-daughter. "At least she didn't die of boredom on an island of small-minded nosybodies!" His eyes blazed as he spoke. "Don't be foolish. This can be your chance. Look at yourself now! You are on the high seas with a father who is daring and brave. A despicable pirate, as you say, but a man people can fear and remember. There are many who would dream of such power and respect. Think of the treasures we can plunder! The dangers we can face! People everywhere will speak of us! Think of how thrilling your life will be far from that placid, dull place. I'll bet even Rosa knew that, too. Why else would she have cast you out to sea? She knew you were destined to be remarkable, to have a life worth living."

With that, Miguel disappeared into the sunlight.

☀ ☀ ☀

It was a long time before Milagros made her way up to the deck to join her father. He stood watching the sun setting on the horizon. She edged closer. Her father's skin glistened with perspiration, and even Milagros could see that her own eyes and dark hair had been presents from him. Yes, he was still a strong and handsome man, a darker, more daring version of the man she had tried to forget. It was as if adventure and daring were seared into every part of him—and his adventure was calling to her now.

Milagros could hear the low thumping of her dinghy against the glorious ship. She admired the rubies along the ship's mast. She ran her hand along the smooth wooden railing, imagining the excitement of racing along this watery world at full mast, throwing caution and manners to the wind.

She took a big breath. She knew what she would do.

Without warning, Milagros scampered onto the railing. Miguel turned at the sound. She wheeled about to face him, legs planted wide. Neither spoke for a moment.

"I don't know whether my mother is alive or dead, Father," Milagros finally said. "I have no water or food, no map to tell me where I am destined. You might be all that I have left, except that dinghy down there."

Miguel flashed a surprised and hopeful smile as he looked up at his daring daughter. His heart began to fill with emotions he had kept secret for years. He would have his little girl once again; she would become his legacy, even if his own deeds were not enough to distinguish him in the lore of evil men. "A wild spirit is never tamed! You'll make a wonderful pirate!" he said triumphantly.

Milagros smiled back. "I *would* be a good pirate, yes. Like any good pirate, I can guess what's in people's hearts, just as you say good pirates can do."

Miguel extended his arm again. "Yes! Yes! It's a gift of the truly adventurous!" Miguel took a step closer.

But Milagros escaped his caress. "Exactly so!" she said. "And that is why I leave you now forever."

With that, she performed a perfect backward dive into the sea.

Miguel ran to the edge of the ship, aghast. He watched the splash ripple out in the water. "Stop! Come back!" he shouted. "What are you doing?"

Milagros emerged breathless near the dinghy and climbed aboard. She untied it and began to row. "I am only doing what you said any good pirate would do. I have read your heart, and it has become a dark stone. Out here, what can a stone do but sink? Besides, you told me all those years ago that it would be up to me to make my way. And now I will—without any help from you. I'm going to find out what happened to my mother."

Miguel reeled back. Rage began to fester in his belly, to disfigure his face. It climbed through his throat and choked out any kind thoughts or hope he had entertained of his only child.

"Bah! She's sitting in the belly of a shark by now!" he called spitefully. "And the same will happen to you, unless other pirates grab you first!"

Milagros paid no heed. She rowed calmly to a rhythm, her boat carving a long V in the surface.

Miguel gave the ship's mast a fierce kick. "You will regret this choice, Milagros! You won't ever forget me or all that would have been yours! Only truly stupid people waste their time on others!" he shouted angrily. He stopped, defeated, watching her grow smaller in the distance. "The truly stupid," he whispered next. "Or, like me, the hopelessly weak."

Miguel scanned the horizon nervously. There was still no sign of his shipmates, who had left him behind as they always did, to mind the ship in their absence like a lowly galley slave. He crossed to the bow and grabbed hold of a large brass ring in the floor. He threw open a hatch door and puffed his chest angrily.

There, bound and gagged, was Rosa, blinking against the bright light. Out of pity, he had bought her from the Rubians, who had sailed by, drunk from celebrating their plunder. She had cost him three slabs of beef and a sack of gold coins he had saved. It was a small fortune by trading standards, all for a stupid woman, a relic of his past he now knew he must forget.

The sight of Rosa in such a pathetic state pinched at his conscience, but he did his best to keep his voice loud and brash like that of all pirates.

"So, that's that, wife. What's done is forever done. She believes me despicable, and so it shall be. Who am I to disappoint her? I will be terrible, awful, despicable." He remembered what his old friends and neighbors had whispered of him. What his father had begged of him: *One must pick something in life and be the very best at it. Can't you do even that?*

Yes, Miguel thought now, *Yes I can. I will be a ruthless pirate—a great disappointment, the greatest disappointment of all.*

He turned again to Rosa. "The others will return soon, and what a surprise you'll be. I know what they whisper about me, Rosa. They think I am too weak to go on our little meetings with other ships, too squeamish to run a knife along a man's bare neck. Good enough only to shine their boots and fetch their food. But you will help me convince them otherwise, Rosa. You can show them how black my heart can be. I can cage my own wife. I can cast my only child out helpless on the sea! I am gloriously hateful!"

Rosa stared into Miguel's face with pity as he spoke. Nothing in her face showed fear, and slowly Miguel could feel his smile fade as she studied him. Now, as always, it was impossible to fool Rosa. She had married him long ago, the only girl willing to look past his father's words at a husband who loved sunsets and hibiscus blooms with the awe of a child. She knew his heart was constricted only by longing and shame, not hate.

Miguel rubbed the back of his neck as his wife gazed at him. In no time, he was wringing his hands, pacing like a worried boy in a costume.

"Why *did* I bother with you at all? Why did I trade food for you? Food *and* gold?" he complained as though it were her fault. He knit his brow as he chewed intently on his bloody fingernails. He knew the answer of course, and the shame of it brought him nearly to madness. In all these years on the seas, he had not been able to cast his conscience to the deep waters. Pieces of it lingered, poking out of the pockets of his mind at the worst possible moments. This cursed remnant of goodness was the reason he had sent the bottled warning to Rosa. It was why he had not let Rosa be caged by the Rubians. It was why even now he wanted Milagros to turn back, to forgive and admire him, to be safe in his care from the horrors of the world.

"They'll throw me from the ship for certain now," he said miserably, realizing at last his costly mistake. He spoke directly to Rosa, his face ashen. "Must I kill you, then? Force you to walk the plank?" But even as he spoke it, he knew he would not have the stomach for such a game. They both knew it was Rosa who had always killed pigs and chickens for their dinner, not he, not even once.

He fell quiet considering his options, pacing around the opening like a rat in a maze. Beads of sweat had formed at his brow.

He scanned the horizon once again. Then he let his eyes rest on his daughter's dinghy growing smaller in the distance. The sun was about to dip into the sea, its reflection igniting the skies into purples and oranges. It was the time of day Miguel most loved, when the sky seemed to throw out its last, futile war whoop before plunging into the ink of night.

But suddenly, Miguel noticed that the water around Milagros was gurgling to life and brightening like lava. A circle of color spread around her, its opaline hues more brilliant than the sky. Miguel squinted, moved to the ship's rail, and held a bejeweled telescope to his eye to get a clearer view.

Stingrays? Curse upon her head: He was sure of it.

He lowered his glass and threw a glance back at the

open hatch door. Carefully, almost terrified of what he might find, Miguel peered below. Rosa's eyes were closed in steady concentration, her face peaceful and calm, lips moving as though in prayer, summoning spirits.

A shiver ran down Miguel's spine. It was a jolt of fear and admiration: for himself embracing wickedness at last, for Rosa and her magic, for his priceless girl, Milagros, now on her journey away from them both.

He slammed the hatch door shut.

CHAPTER 12

The Rescue

How will I die out here?

That's what Milagros wondered as she bobbed along the vast sea for days on end. It was the specifics that intrigued her. Would she blister to death in the scorching sun? Would an enormous shark bump her into the sea? Or would she die in a churning storm?

To pass the long hours between periods of sleep, she counted how many rays, and what kinds, were following her. The number always changed, but she never had fewer than a dozen companions. "Where am I?" she asked them, but she never received a reply.

Soon her stomach growled and her lips cracked. She drained the last bottle of water that had been stored beneath the seat and took to sleeping most of the day, curled into a ball with her face down to escape the searing sun that shrank her skin against her bones. *It will be this way, then*, she thought as she prepared to die of thirst and hunger: a torrid sleep with her eyes open in terrible dreams of all that had happened in Las Brisas. Then, a slip into blackness.

She did not realize, of course, that there are many kinds of death, some to be endured while we are very much alive. For a girl who has lost her home and family, there are more ways to become a ghost than there are fish in all the seas.

☀ ☀ ☀

She was roused from her stupor by her dinghy's sharp lurch. She opened her eyes and noticed a strange sensation. Her nose was running, and her skin was the gooseflesh of those plagued by fever. But as she awakened further, she saw that the tips of her stiff fingers looked blue.

Milagros uncurled herself like an arthritic old woman, and with every ounce of remaining energy, she grabbed hold of the sides of her dinghy and peered out. The warm, clear waters she had been traveling were gone. All around her were frothy waves that heaved her boat forward with brutal force. A mountainous swell, heavy with seaweed, crashed inside her boat, and the icy sting made her shout with the last trace of her voice.

"*¡Ay!*" she sputtered, just as another wave heaved her high into the air.

Then a sight ahead made her gasp. She was no longer far out in the ocean. Instead, her tiny boat was being hurled closer to jagged cliffs covered in moss and capped by snow. Huge sprays of saltwater erupted each time a wave crashed against the rocks. She was about to be dashed to pieces.

"Help!" she cried to anyone in the world, to God, to the stingrays. She squeezed shut her eyes as her boat slammed down near rocks that jutted all around her like a beast's teeth. The wood beneath her feet creaked. Her clothes were soaked, and she shivered with a cold in her bones she had never known before.

Then, a shout made her look up. Tucked high at the top of the cliff was a wooden house. It was the faded gray of a memory, pointy-topped, with two windows like eyes in a sad face. Smoke curled upward from its stone chimney.

A man waved his arms in her direction. At his heels, a shaggy white dog barked and circled, urgently announcing trouble.

"Help!" she screamed again as the nose of the dinghy banged against a ledge.

The man rushed back inside. A moment later, he

reappeared, pulling on a jacket and clutching a thick coil of rope in one hand. He held tight to his hat against the stiff wind as he descended the slippery incline. Behind him was a woman in a bright green sweater with blankets in her arms; she was pulling along a small blond girl. Together they climbed down along the widest part of the treacherous rocks, cautious of the deep crevices that plunged to the sea.

Milagros was surrounded everywhere now by sharp ledges and swirling eddies; the cliff face, almost vertical, loomed an arm's-reach away. She watched in horror as yet another wave threw her high into the air. This time, she felt her body lift from the dinghy floor. Her hands lost their grip, and Milagros was flung into the angry water. Her body slammed against the rock wall. Warm blood filled her mouth as she sank with the weight of a stone.

Las Brisas was burning. Ash floated in black flakes to the white sand. The smell of her mother's groves aflame made Milagros scream.

"Mamá!" she cried.

But when she opened her eyes and looked around her, she found that the scent of burning wood was not the apocalypse she had only recently escaped.

It was a fireplace where several cats lay napping, one ear alert for good measure. A tomcat, disturbed, hissed a warning at her.

With the stillness of an iguana, Milagros looked around the dark room that smelled of a damp cellar. The walls were crowded with crooked paintings of every size: lighthouses, sea stars, boats with their sterns low in the water. On the mantel she spied fishing nets, driftwood, and old buoys.

Just then, a cold snout pushed against her sore neck and a rough tongue licked at her earlobes.

"Off, Mollie," a voice ordered.

Milagros bolted up painfully—her whole body felt bruised—as the shaggy dog retreated to a man who was sitting across from her. He watched her keenly as he stroked the downy yellow braids of a girl who sat on the arm of his easy chair. With a trim beard and rimless glasses, he looked like a young sea captain. His hair was an inky black, wet like her own, Milagros noted. Clearly he had plunged in after her.

"You'll need dry clothes," he said. "We're looking now."

English, Milagros thought. She craned her neck toward the window that rattled softly in the wind. The sky was the featureless gray of smoke. Where was she?

Somewhere north, certainly. It was obvious from the cold, from the man's language.

"Doesn't she talk?"

The girl had the man's clear blue eyes, but none of their softness. She gazed at Milagros for a moment and gathered a cat in her arms to nuzzle its neck by the fire. "It's rude not to speak to the people who save you," she muttered to no one in particular.

Milagros ignored her and stared once again out the window. The man followed her gaze.

"You're in Holly Pointe, miss," he said. "Between Maine and nowhere," he added with a shrug, "which suits most of us fine." He extended his hand. It was calloused, a bear's paw. "I'm John Winters. And this is my daughter, Diana."

Milagros sat back, stunned. The coast of the North Atlantic? Impossible! How could she have drifted such a distance? How long could she have slept at sea?

"Do you have a name?" John asked at last.

Milagros turned to him, trying to read his heart as best she could. Behind the glitter of his pupils was a shard of sadness, the kind that could make a man into a monster over time. She would have to be cautious.

"Maybe she's deaf," Diana whispered into her father's ear.

Milagros tried to straighten her shoulders.

"*Me llamo Milagros*," she croaked. And then, because the girl's surprised look gave her courage, she added in the English Señorita Alma had taught her, "My name is Milagros." She paused. "*Miracle* in your tongue."

John leaned back and pulled at his beard. A small smile was forcing the corner of his lips.

"Well," he said, thinking. "That's a fine name. Reminds me of one of the best men I ever knew. His was a skiff named *Miracle*."

His eyes fell on Milagros's bare feet, the blue tinge of her nails, the welts forming around her ankles. His expression darkened.

"No soul should be out in February waters, Miracle. What happened to you and the others? Caught in a bad blow?"

Others.

She thought of Señorita Alma and Dr. López, lifeless in the groves. She heard Rosa's voice urging her to run. Her throat grew dry once again, and she pulled her wet blankets close.

"There are no others," she said.

Before John could reply, the woman from the cliff rushed in, talking hurriedly as she held up pants and a sweater. "These don't fit Diana yet. Let's get her into them." She stopped, holding her breath when she saw

Milagros sitting up. The woman was unkempt and dressed in the colors of a new spring day. Her short, unruly hair hung in her moon face, and her hands, marked by long shapely fingers, were stained everywhere with dabs of dirt and paint. She walked slowly toward Milagros and pushed back her ratted hair.

"A girl from the sea," she whispered, smiling. "How very marvelous." She knelt at Milagros's feet to inspect for frostbite. "Do you mind?"

"My wife, Patty," John explained. He crossed to the window and turned to his wife. "The girl says there are no others." He listened again to the groan of the wind outside. "There's no one else out there that I can see. Not even debris." He lowered his voice and set his jaw. "Who would let a child leave the mainland alone?" he asked.

Patty stopped rubbing and looked into Milagros's eyes. "Maybe she's not from the mainland, John."

"No? Where from then?"

"Somewhere farther Away," Patty said vaguely. She winked at Milagros. "From the place where mermaids live, I suppose."

John glanced over his shoulder at his wife, and they both broke into a smile.

Diana's eyes darted from one parent to the other. "Mermaids aren't real," she corrected. "And Away people are wicked."

Patty pursed her lips and kept working, ignoring the smudges of oil paints she had smeared all over Milagros's feet. When she was through, she handed Milagros the dry clothes and pointed down a narrow hall.

"Change in the room down there. You'll feel better after a warm bath."

Milagros hobbled down the hallway on prickly feet, her head throbbing with pain. She had just reached the door when she stopped at a small painting among the multitude that crowded the wall. All the paintings were brilliant furors of color, but this one in particular drew her attention. No larger than a shoe box, it was a canvas of a vibrant ocean churning against a cliff. Rising from its center was a mermaid whose hair hung in tendrils to the heart-shaped slope of her tail. A red mist filled the sky.

Milagros closed the bathroom door and studied her calloused face and swollen lip in the mirror. Carefully, she peeled away the remains of her wet clothes. They had been reduced to nothing more than a second skin reeking of fish and sorrow. She arranged them lovingly on the floor like the clothes of a paper doll. They were all that was left of the girl she knew herself to be.

A voice whispering beneath the door interrupted her.

"You can't stay here," Diana said. "Go back to Away."

CHAPTER 13

The Girl from Away

No one came forward to claim her.

John heated fish soup and oyster crackers and proudly taught her the names of all the hissing feral cats—dozens upon dozens—that he fed lovingly among the rusted debris in his front yard. Patty drew sketches of her face for the ferry captain, for the postmistress, for anyone who might recognize those intelligent features and find the family that had lost their child. Diana watched in agony as her besotted parents grew more enraptured by the sparkle of their new orphan. In a matter of days, she emptied a bureau drawer of her belongings and her heart of all goodwill for Milagros.

"It's never too much bother to help someone in need," Patty told her quietly when Diana complained.

"It's only until her own family finds her again," John added. "We'll help her get back on her feet."

Milagros, listening quietly behind doors, understood every word. Señorita Alma had given her a key to unlock this mysterious world, but now English felt like fire to her ears.

She wandered inside the Winterses' drafty house for weeks, wondering whether Diana alone had sense enough to suspect the terrible truth.

No one was ever going to come for Milagros.

※ ※ ※

"Here we are," John announced as he pulled to a squeaky stop before a faded cedar building. Milagros, sufficiently recuperated, sat shivering between him and Patty. White puffs of breath were the only sure sign that she had not frozen to death on the way back from taking Diana to school. The borrowed coat and mittens Milagros wore left her wrists exposed to the alarming cold. It was early March, but who could have recognized it as such? At home, March was marked by butterfly jasmine perfuming the night air. But here, the trees were still forlorn sticks, and the only scent lingering was that of fishy clam flats. That morning the thermometer had been lodged at ten degrees, the warmest day in more than a month.

Now as they huddled inside the old truck for heat, Patty pointed out the important landmarks, many of which Milagros recognized from Patty's paintings: squat buildings whose reflections rippled in the oily water beneath the pier; worn lobster boats, handed down from father to son, floating among the ice chunks that crowded their slips; the bait-and-gear shack; a tailor-and-mending store for both sails and clothing. To Milagros, the abandoned street was the coldest and ugliest place in the world.

She thought of Patty's paintings, glowing like finches in a gardenia bush. Lies.

"Everything here is the color of ash," she complained.

Patty's eyes sparkled. "Oh, no. There's color in every place," she said, sliding out of the truck. "You just need to know how to look."

"We're late," John said. He climbed up the plank steps two at a time. Mollie, who had been riding happily in back, bounded through the door he held open.

The lobstermen who idled during the winter months at the coffee counter turned at the sound of their footsteps. Even perched at their stools, their cautious eyes darted nervously in the habit of fishermen who must work between the tempestuous sky and sea. The men's hands made their mugs look like demitasses, huge hands, rough from scraping barnacles and hauling heavy traps over the sides of their boats. Their hands were twice the size of John's, the island handyman. They grunted a welcome at John and Patty, who were already making their way to a small table at the back of the room. Milagros pulled her tight coat closed and hurried behind Patty's bright orange parka. The largest man of all, the one who had summoned them, was standing at his table, waiting.

Officer Ned Granger, Holly Pointe's only policeman, ran his fingers along his rusted handcuffs as Milagros spoke. He was pale, with a shock of red hair and silver eyes that gave him the empty expression of a cod.

He picked at his teeth with the corner of a sugar packet as she told about the Rubians, glanced carelessly at Patty's atlas where Milagros pointed at the precise place of her home, snorted when she told them she might be the last Brisenian alive. She had not been able to summon the strength to mention Rosa's magic or the mantas. The words to describe magic in so barren a place withered on her lips. English, she realized now, was too limited to capture it. *What's the use*, she reasoned, staring into Ned Granger's blank face. He was simply an armed man with no good sense—always a most dangerous combination in her view.

"Away people," he muttered, shaking his head. "If

they're not ruining an island with motorboats and fancy houses, they're casting off their lunatics."

Milagros gave him an ugly stare, even as John's arm slipped around her shoulder.

Mrs. Mildred Mulligan, a schoolteacher who had accompanied Ned Granger, nodded emphatically. She was an older woman in heavy boots and gray flannel slacks that matched her coarse hair. She had come in place of the obvious choice of helpers, the island's seamstress—the only other resident to have ever lived Away—but who was, unfortunately, visiting relatives. Mrs. Mulligan glanced anxiously at her watch. She had left her class in the care of an alarmingly young substitute.

"Ned's right," Mrs. Mulligan said. "They think we believe in their fish tales. She needs to be turned over to the mainland authorities at once."

Milagros's old fire had been stoked. She stood up with a start.

"I am not a lunatic, *señora*," she blurted out. "And not a liar."

Mrs. Mulligan tightened her shriveled lips and exchanged a knowing glance with Ned Granger.

"Little girls float to our shores from tropical seas, do they? Without a drop of water or food? From places that are not on any map?"

Milagros leaned over the atlas that Patty had so

carefully pulled from her bookshelves. She stabbed her finger at the blank spot marking the precise latitude and longitude where she had most certainly lived all her life.

"It is not on this map, madam," Milagros conceded in the formal tone Señorita Alma had always recommended for debating contentious points. "But that is unimportant. Maps are full of mistakes. Look." She balled her fists and measured the continents' relative sizes. "North America is far too big. Two countries in Africa have their old names. The new nations of Europe don't appear." She shook her head and swallowed the knot that was forming in her throat. She knew Señorita Alma would have been appalled at Mrs. Mulligan's shabby understanding of cartography, if not proud of Milagros's logic and language skills.

"The real world is much more complicated than any map," she concluded. She pushed back the atlas and held Mrs. Mulligan's stony gaze. "Forgive me, but you should know that. You're a teacher."

Mildred Mulligan's hand went to her neck as if to protect herself from a strangler. John let out a chuckle.

"Stay calm, Mildred," he said gently. "Dr. Hughes has already warned you about agitations." He guided Milagros back to her chair. "It makes no difference where Away is, does it? At least not to me and Patty. Here or Away, a child is not something to throw out when it's inconvenient. I know *you* understand that better than anyone."

Mrs. Mulligan pursed her lips and looked at her fingernails uncomfortably. "I do," she admitted.

"Then she stays," he said happily. "At least for now."

Ned Granger leaned forward on his massive elbows. "Listen to reason, John. There's none of us who can solve every trouble the world belches up on our rocks. Smart people learn to worry about their own problems."

John crossed his arms. "A child is not a problem," he said. "And what's the rush? Her parents could very well turn up in time."

An uncomfortable silence fell on the group.

Finally, Patty took John's hand and smiled. "Or maybe, she is just meant to be here for a while."

Ned Granger sat back and sighed. They had been friends since the days of shooting marbles and netting sardines off the pier. It was easier to grow gills than to change John Winters's mind.

"You're as stubborn a pair of islanders as there ever was," he told them.

John smiled. "Thank you, Ned."

The policeman stood and made his way toward the door, the matter temporarily settled in his mind.

"I'll see you back to the schoolhouse, Mildred." He set his police hat on his head and turned to them all. "I'll let it rest for now. But contrary to popular opinion, John, even in Holly Pointe we have rules. It can't go on like this forever."

Patty helped Mrs. Mulligan with her quilted coat.

"Can't we talk some good sense into you?" Mrs. Mulligan whispered to her as she pulled on her scarf, hat, and gloves. When she was through, she had the appearance of an Eskimo.

"Good sense?" Patty's eyes flashed. "How would that help? We've received a Miracle. What we need is faith."

Mrs. Mulligan tucked her hands in her pockets and drew them out with a look of surprise. Sugar sifted through her gloved fingers to the floor. "What on earth—"

You are certainly in need of sweetening, Milagros thought wickedly, hiding the empty packets under her foot. She pulled on her own coat as Mrs. Mulligan shook out her pocket and cast a dubious glance in her direction.

"Both of you are too kind for this world. Always have been. If you ask me, she's been abandoned by some rogue at the Brookhaven Pier. You'll see that I'm right. Lazy drunkards, the whole lot, this time of year," she muttered. "Busy with nothing but regrets, whiskey, and stories of pirates stealing children into the mist."

Milagros stopped buttoning. "Pirates?"

Her voice echoed in the room, but no one except Mollie, whose tail curled between her legs, seemed to hear. Milagros thought at once of her father's ferocious temper and his ugly warnings as she had deserted him. Would Miguel de la Torre, in his rage, send pirates to seek revenge? Would he harm his own child?

Cold and dread made Milagros tremble as Ned Granger pulled open the door to a wind that bit into the marrow of her bones. His expression was somber as he searched the sky.

"No one comes out of thin air, Patty. This child is not like one of your paintings, dropped on us from your imagination. Sooner or later, you'll both have to ask yourselves, *Who is this girl? Where does she really belong?*"

The words hung in the air long after the door banged shut and the sound of tires on the gravel driveway faded.

On the way home, Patty tried to build cheer by drawing mermaids in the steamed panes as John told jokes. But Milagros's mind had traveled far away.

Who is this girl? Where does she belong?

She had no answer for herself. Here in Holly Pointe there was no Rosa or Señorita Alma to help light the way. No dusty avocado bins or macaws perched in living room windows. No magic or color of any kind. There was only a new girl named Miracle stranded in a place of wicked cold and the threat of pirates waiting for her in the mist.

As their truck struggled up the precarious cliffs toward home, Milagros turned to listen to the first long blast of a foghorn that sounded mournfully over the water. Behind them, a heavy mist was rolling in across the land. Mollie circled in the flatbed nervously and growled. Soon Holly Pointe was hidden inside the ghostly folds.

CHAPTER 14

The Ship's Slave

What is more dangerous than an evil man?

A weak and fearful one. There is no telling what terrible actions such a man will set in motion to quiet the scary creatures he thinks are snapping at his heels.

This is what Rosa decided about Miguel as she dragged a mop across the floorboards of the *Ruby Sails*. She had been scrubbing floors, mending clothes, and preparing meals on the ship for weeks. Miguel had finally convinced El Capitán to make her the ship's servant, a job that, to Miguel's great shock and disappointment, had been his own when he had first set sail from Las Brisas.

El Capitán had his doubts.

"Make her useful," he had said carefully. "She dies as soon as she's not, De la Torre."

Since then, she had been tethered by one ankle to a

long chain that made a terrible scraping sound as she dragged it from one side of the ship to the other doing her chores. She slept curled up like a stray dog with no protection from windy nights or rain.

¡Ay! Handsome Miguel had been her ruin after all. What would her sweet grandfather make of this now? Rosa wondered miserably. Don Antonio had been such an honorable man, with friends throughout the island who left flowers outside their home when he had finally died at one hundred.

"In life and in farming, Rosita, you must always carry two baskets," don Antonio had told her when the farm was new and she was just a girl. "One to hold the good seeds that you will plant with care, and the other to collect the fruits that you will sow from your kind labor."

His self-confidence and goodness had left Rosa unprepared for Miguel. He had not told her that some seeds, like Miguel, would not bear fruit. That no seed grows if it cannot feel the sunny heat of hope in its roots.

She had loved Miguel, but so often she was alone in this. Only she seemed to appreciate how intoxicated he became by simple things, like a rising moon or the smell of gardenias in the air. No one applauded him for his patience and tenderness with Milagros. Instead, they saw a man who was lazy and dreamy. In the end, Miguel had believed them. He had chosen the short and familiar road that his neighbors had carefully marked for him his whole life: the road to spectacular failure.

Who was paying the price for everyone's cruelty now? Milagros, the most innocent victim of all. Rosa's face burned in anger.

Her ankle throbbed. It was red and sore, growing more infected each day. She gazed up at the lookout perched in the crow's nest and then at the sky. By the position of the sun, she estimated the time to be about four o'clock, still several hours before the last lookout would climb from his perch and head down below. She could wait, she told herself. She'd have to think about something other than her painful leg for just a while longer, just until dark when sleep blanketed the ship. It was then that Miguel would sneak to her with a cup of saltwater to clean out her wound. Silently, his gentle eyes averted, he would pour water over her sores and pat her ankle dry with a rough towel. It hurt for a moment, and several times she had almost cried out. But at least the saltwater would help ease her pain and let her rest.

Rest, yes, she thought. *But not sleep.* Nightmares plagued Rosa now, and the thought of her eyes drifting shut gave her the sensation of being closed up in a box of horrors. She imagined Milagros drowning, as Rosa's own parents had, in a great swell of water. She could hear the cracking of bones as a sea monster clamped down on the girl's legs. She felt the presence of birds hovering, waiting patiently for the girl's death before plucking at her remains.

Rosa ran the mop back and forth in a rhythm toward the bow, concentrating her thoughts on the swaying of the mop and on the manta rays she had trusted. *Uno-dos-tres.* Mi-la-gros. Mi-la-gros. Mi-la-gros. She stopped for a moment to peer into the water. She closed her tired eyes and concentrated on her only hope. Nothing. Would she never get word?

She pressed the mop more firmly into the floor-boards and began to make her way back. As she turned, her mop hit a small object and sent it spinning away. Rosa scanned the deck to see what it was. Out of the corner of her eye, she saw it: a bright red bottle, the very kind that Milagros had found.

Rosa's mind raced as she put her head down and mopped her way toward the bottle. Her heart beat faster. Miguel's message had reached her. Couldn't another message reach Milagros? Perhaps she could use the hem of her dress as paper, even drops of her own blood as ink— anything to place a message inside. *Milagros! I am alive, captive on the* Ruby Sails. *I will find you again if I can. Do not despair! I am coming!*

She made her way to the corner of the deck where the bottle rolled gently with the sway of the ship. Carefully, she pushed her bucket to wedge the bottle in a corner. She dipped her mop in the water and bent down as if to wring it. Now was her chance. She reached toward the red glass.

A dirty hand grabbed her wrist. "What do you think you're doing, woman?"

Miguel stood with his legs apart, an angry scowl on his face. The lookout glanced at the disturbance on the deck and turned his lazy eyes back to the horizon. Rosa straightened at once as Miguel picked up the bottle and slid it inside the pocket of his trousers.

Rosa's heart shriveled. "I was only cleaning up, husband," she said in a defeated whisper.

"Don't call me husband on this ship or I will throw you overboard this minute," he hissed, looking over his shoulder.

She fell silent as Miguel looked out over the water.

"She is surely dead," Miguel mumbled.

Rosa closed her eyes to listen. She heard a glimmer of regret in his voice. It was banging in his chest like a bird against a glass. Perhaps it was not too late.

"Miguel," she began cautiously. "She is our child. If she is dead, there is nothing to do but mourn her and our mistakes all of our days. But if she is alive and does not know my end, it is worse."

Miguel glanced at her from the corner of his eye. "Worse?"

"Yes, worse. Do you know what it is to wonder whether one is motherless, Miguel? It is to be waiting forever. It is to have no mirror of the past to help shape the future. It is to be afraid to have hope for oneself, Miguel. You, more than anyone, know how terrible a curse hopelessness can be."

For a moment, Miguel's eyes grew large. His mouth hung open, and Rosa's heart brightened at the thought that perhaps she had reached the part of Miguel he was trying so desperately to kill.

Miguel's face twisted in agony. "Stop talking to me as if I am still the man of long ago. That man is dead."

"I don't believe you," Rosa whispered. "Goodness is still inside you, Miguel. There is still time."

Miguel shook his head fiercely and bared his teeth.

"Silence! It is too late, Rosa. I have made my choice." He took in a deep breath and forced his face into a brave scowl. "Milagros is no longer of any consequence to me at all," he said from behind eyes that looked anguished. "None. One insolent girl is either suffering or gone. *Pfft!*"—he snapped his finger. "What does it matter?"

Miguel did not wait for a reply. He stormed off, the

red bottle protruding from his pocket. It caught the light with each angry stride.

※ ※ ※

For three nights, Miguel did not come to soak Rosa's ankle, and it swelled painfully against the metal cuff. Discomfort and worry would not let her sleep. She lay on the floor of the deck uncomfortably.

The men had long ago gone to their quarters. The full moon shimmered across the ocean as she talked into the air. "Will I never see her again?"

There came a loud yelling.

"*¡Vete!—¡vete de aquí!*" Go on! Get out of here!

It was Miguel's voice, loud and slurred.

"I'll kill the man who's ruined my sleep," thundered El Capitán as he rushed on deck followed by two sleepy men who were naked to the waist.

There in the moonlight stood Miguel, drunk, shaking his fists at something in the water.

"Shut up, you foul drunk, before I have your head on a pike," El Capitán ordered.

But Miguel paid no mind. "*¡Vete, Diablo!* Go away, Devil!" he shouted again.

Rosa slid herself to the edge of the ship as quietly as her chain would allow. She winced in pain as she strained to see the cause of Miguel's fury. The moonlight lit the shimmering water, and Rosa saw immediately the source of his rage. There beneath the boat was an enormous black manta ray, swimming in circles, shooting itself out of the water as if it were a dolphin. With each lurch from the water, it opened its fins wide—the length of three men standing head to toe. It hovered for a moment, its solid black eyes fixed on Miguel, before crashing into the water again.

Rosa gasped. Surely, there was a message for her. But what? The chains bound her painfully to her spot. The men, now roused from their beds, stepped over her carelessly, their laughter ringing out across the ship.

"I am here," Rosa called toward the manta ray. But no one heard her over the laughter and shouting, and the manta continued its furious display. *What do you need to tell me?* she thought desperately. *Is she alive? Is she well?*

Miguel shook his fist in a rage. Something in his hand caught the white moonlight. It was the bottle, the very bottle he had taken from Rosa three days before. As she watched in horror, he hurled it at the beast with all his might.

The manta shuddered as the glass hit its snout and made a gash in its skin. In a moment, it lay utterly still in the water and then slowly sank into the blackness.

Miguel fell to his knees, crying as his shipmates jeered.

"¡*Bravo*! ¡*Arriba*! Here's to Miguel, that brave fish fighter of the high seas."

"Go to sleep, you drunk idiot," ordered El Capitán with a look of disgust on his face. He had never thought Miguel worthy of a pirate's fearsome name. "Go back to sleep, all of you!"

Miguel looked up at the captain, his body spent and his face filled with dread. It was as though he had fought for his very soul. He wiped his nose with the back of his hand and stumbled toward the sleeping quarters below.

"*Bruja*," Miguel whispered as he stumbled past Rosa. Witch. Tears were in his eyes. "I have done as you have bid me."

Rosa had no time to consider Miguel's cryptic words. She closed her eyes and pretended to sleep as the rest of the men made their way past her again. El Capitán paused for a moment where she lay. As their footsteps finally faded, she strained her ears for the tiniest splash. She concentrated all her thoughts on the manta.

But for the rest of the night, and for many, many weeks afterward, there was not a single sound. Instead, a deathly silence engulfed the ship. Whatever message had been meant for her, Rosa knew it was now lost forever at the bottom of the sea.

CHAPTER 15

Pirate Dreams

That very night, Milagros lay in bed studying the same multitude of stars that guided the *Ruby Sails*. Sleep would not take her by the hand, and all she could do was close her eyes and wonder where she might go when the truth about her parents became clear.

"You're the fortunate girl," Patty whispered to Diana, thinking Milagros asleep. "You have a warm house and parents who love you. She has nothing."

"Daddy always takes care of what other people don't want," Diana said. "Why? Am I not enough?"

"Shh, shh, shh," Patty replied gently, kissing Diana's eyes.

Milagros tried to hear only the crash of the surf below. It was nothing like the lullabies of Las Brisas: frogs making a racket, birds of every variety chattering in their nests. Instead, the sound was violent and it lured her mind to the place of her worst fears.

As the hours ticked by, her doubts emerged boldly from their favorite hiding places in the dark corners of the night. They danced in frenzy with Diana's careless words. And then, victorious, they made a new truth take hold.

Rosa had not wanted her own child. She never had.

In the end, Rosa had simply abandoned her, Milagros now knew. She had cast Milagros out to the sea to fend for herself with an empty promise that she'd somehow survive. In reality, she had let her only child go the way people left behind the wild cats that prowled the Winterses' yard searching for scraps. What kind of mother did such a thing?

A bad one. A mother with a barren heart.

Growing plants, homegrown remedies—Rosa's qualities seemed meaningless now. *Yes*, Milagros thought, *Rosa was just the hopelessly useless mother the townspeople always said she was.* Both her parents were failures. One was an eccentric and the other a scoundrel. Her suffering was entirely their fault.

She slipped into the fitful sleep of those who fear they are unloved. But just as she teetered on the edge of that desperate pit, a bloodcurdling scream pierced the air. It came from outside her window, high-pitched and pained, the shriek of a woman's soul being torn from her body.

At first, Milagros did not dare move. But when a second screech erupted, she was sure she was not dreaming. She wrapped her quilt at her shoulders and went to the window to see the trouble. The moon and stars had been swallowed by clouds, and nothing was visible except the whitecaps smashing against the rocks. But far off on the other side of the island, the lighthouse beacon sent a beam over the ocean. In each pulse of light, she saw a thick blanket of fog creeping in long tendrils toward the island. But tonight the fog was different, more menacing, and as she watched, men's faces took shape inside the moving mist.

Milagros, they seemed to call in a ghastly serenade.

Pirates. Surely, they had been loosened upon her by Miguel.

Diana stirred and rubbed her eyes groggily. For a moment, Milagros felt relief even in this companionship.

"Do you hear that?" Milagros asked her. "The screams?"

Diana turned her back.

"They hate you," Diana whispered from her own troubled dreams. "They want you to go away."

Milagros fumbled back in the darkness and pulled

the covers over her cold shoulders. All night the pirates taunted her and cackled, but she refused to close her eyes or cower in fear.

When the sun rose at last and cast lavender streaks over the sky, she was still awake, her hair wet with perspiration and her temples throbbing. She had completed her defiant vigil and felt safe now that the light of the world had chased the world's darkest thoughts back to the bottom of the sea.

From the living room came the comforting sounds of John starting the morning fire.

She rose slowly and looked outside. The sight ahead made her heart squeeze in horror.

"John!" she screamed. "John!"

Clumps of fur blew like tumbleweeds in the wind. Mollie lay bloodied and still on the rocks.

CHAPTER 16

Healer

Dread rooted Milagros to her spot in the kitchen as everyone around her sprang into action.

In a flash, John was outside. He shouted for Patty, who ran barefoot to join him, and together they wrapped Mollie in a blanket, lifting her away from the cats who circled her wildly, hissing and swatting at their legs.

John kicked the door ajar. The dog's wounds were deep, and clotted dark blood dripped along the floor. Something had tried to rip Mollie's legs to shreds. Her eyes were wide and fixed; her tongue lolled to one side.

Diana screamed at the sight.

"Hush, now," Patty ordered. She ransacked the cabinets, cursing under her breath, until at last she found an old box marked with a red cross. She pulled out a roll of gauze and began tearing strips with her teeth.

"Lay her here," she said. John placed Mollie gently on the floor, and the two set to work.

"What would do this terrible thing?" she muttered, grimacing as she examined the dog, scarcely knowing where to begin. She felt for a heartbeat. "Did you hear anything last night?"

Milagros wanted to tell them about the mist, about the pirates cackling, but how could she without sounding foolish? And worse, how could she tell them that their sweet dog had been savaged on her own father's orders?

She edged slowly into the room. She knew the high price of keeping important secrets; she had paid dearly for one already. The truth had to be told.

"There was a scream," she began.

John turned. "A scream?"

Milagros nodded. Her heart pounded in fear as she tried to find words to shape the truth. "Yes. In the night, like a woman wailing. It was—"

"Fishers," John blurted out. "Damn nuisance."

Diana cut in with another screech. "A fisher killed Mollie?" She put her face in her hands and sobbed.

Patty kept her eyes on her work. She dabbed at the cuts gingerly. "Quiet! We can't help Mollie unless we can hear ourselves think."

Milagros fell silent. John had told her about the nasty martens before. Weasel-like in appearance, fishers had sharp teeth and endless appetites for the cats that prowled the rocks at night.

Mollie is too large for a fisher, she thought. No. Something else, something ugly and darkly magical had hurt Mollie.

Patty stopped her work to listen again for the dog's heartbeat.

"She's barely breathing, John. I'm afraid she won't make it to the mainland."

John moved to her side.

"Let me try." He took up dabbing the oozing wounds. "Come on, old girl. You're all right. Come on, Mollie." His face was a combination of determination and despair.

For all his effort, however, Mollie's spirit was pulling away. The dog's body was stiff, and her chest moved only sporadically. Patty reached for Diana, whose howls now filled the kitchen.

Suddenly, Milagros had an idea.

She rushed back to her bedroom and crossed to the dresser that Diana had so reluctantly shared with her. She dug quickly through her clothes and found the rusted tin of Rosa's salve at the bottom of the drawer. Opening it, she paused. She had never healed anyone herself. She had only accompanied her mother, carried

Rosa's satchel, and fetched herbs that were pointed out to her on their walks. It was Rosa who understood the secret needs of the ill. There was no other choice but to try, Milagros decided. Perhaps Rosa's magic would be powerful enough now. Perhaps in this at least her mother could prove useful.

She grabbed the tin and ran back to the kitchen. Without hesitation, she fell to her knees at John's side. "Here," she said, thrusting the tin at him.

"What do you think you're doing?" Diana shouted.

"Saving Mollie," Milagros snapped.

Patty looked at the tin in Milagros's hand and then at John. "What is it?"

"I don't know," Milagros admitted. "But it's from home. It belonged to my—" She could not tell them about Rosa now. "It's powerful."

"Don't let her touch Mollie," Diana screamed. "She'll make it worse!"

"Quickly!" Milagros told John. "Don't wait. Let me try."

"No!" Diana pulled the tin from Milagros's hands.

John turned to Diana and spoke more sharply than Milagros had ever heard. His voice cracked with frustration. "There's nothing else to do, Diana. It's this or fold our hands and watch Mollie die."

Milagros took back the salve. With trembling fingers,

she scooped out the thick paste and swabbed the wounds.

It seemed an eternity that they waited in silence as Mollie lay perfectly still.

Despair wrapped Milagros. She closed her eyes, the way her mother often did when she was healing others. She had never asked Rosa what she thought of during those times of meditation. She had assumed it was an incantation or prayer, something far beyond the reach of ordinary people like her. But now Milagros found that her own thoughts were urgent. She could not fail against the pirates' murderous prank, especially not in front of Diana, who expected her—*wanted* her in some way—to falter.

And then it happened.

The silence began to pull Milagros away to a place past ordinary wishes where she could imagine Mollie wagging her tail, racing after John to leap inside his truck.

How long she stood dreaming in this way would always be a mystery to Milagros. But soon enough a weak growl broke the stillness and pulled her back to the kitchen. Milagros opened her eyes with a start and held her breath. Mollie's chest lifted and fell ever so slightly; her hind legs twitched. At the edge of the deepest wound, a scab began binding over the blood.

A look of awe spread across John's face as he ran his forefinger over Mollie's nose. The dog was still on her side, but the wounds had ceased bleeding, and her eyes lost their blankness. She gave a tired whine.

Patty's eyes grew wide as she watched each cut close. She put her ear to the dog's chest and then turned to Milagros, wary and speechless.

"It's incredible," she said at last. She turned to Diana. "Come look, Diana. Mollie's getting well."

Diana approached and gave Mollie's ear a gentle scratch. Then she looked up, her eyes filled with a mix of fear and resentment. She pushed past Milagros without a word. The windows rattled loudly as she slammed her bedroom door in defeat.

CHAPTER 17

Messages

In the weeks that followed the attack, Milagros brushed aside Diana's hateful stares. More important work was at hand for a girl who had glimpsed the face of vengeance and had battled it with her magic.

By day, she tended Mollie's wounds faithfully. But at night, when the blast of the foghorn sounded, she took a seat at her window and waited eagerly for the pirate ghosts to begin their ruckus. She was determined not to cower in fear. Instead, she armed herself with curses she invented and angry messages that she hoped they would take back to Miguel, their puppeteer.

But night after night, to her disappointment, no ghosts returned. Holly Pointe's fog remained the harmless cotton gauze of John and Patty's happy dreams.

Milagros paced and pondered.

She knew better than to trust the crafty silence of

evil. If she stayed in Holly Pointe, pirate ghosts would surely return, and who could say where their malice would end? Above all, she wanted no harm to come to John or Patty, who had treated her with kindness.

One morning, then, rising from the chair where she dozed during her nightly watch, she made her decision. She would have no choice but to leave Holly Pointe. Turning to her trusty companions with the confidence of a priestess at the altar, she closed her eyes and called out over the sea with her heart's strong song. *Come back to me*, she ordered.

Unfortunately, a most inconvenient complication arose. Ned Granger arrived at their kitchen that afternoon in April, his chest bulging with his new and disastrous plans.

"We're not a place that likes to promote ignorance among children," the officer said in an imitation of compassion. "You do understand that, don't you?"

Weary of John's excuses, he had arrived unexpectedly, betting in favor of the element of surprise. If the Away Girl were to stay in Holly Pointe, he explained, she would be required to enroll in school like every other respectable child on the island. "She'll finish the remaining two months of the term, with the superintendent's permission. Starts May first."

Milagros spied the word *unknown* under the box marked PARENTS on the registration forms Ned Granger had so cleverly thought to bring along. She felt ill at the thought of school. She had never liked being among classmates who feared her. It would be no different here, maybe worse with Diana as a classmate.

No matter, she told herself, stifling a yawn. May was still a few weeks away. She would be long gone before anyone would be calling her name on the roster.

"Fishers." Ned Granger grunted. He looked out the window at Mollie, who was sniffing around crocuses that were erupting through the cracks in the cliffs. "Worse than ever this year. Emma Eustis has lost three kittens this month alone."

Milagros dried her hands at the sink and returned the empty tin of her mother's salve to her pocket. She had helped John unravel the last of Mollie's dirty bandages only moments before the policeman's arrival. She couldn't help but feel proud about Mollie. Only the tiniest limp remained as she nosed nervously among the bright azalea buds. Milagros smiled to herself. She had worked so tirelessly on saving the dog that she had not, until now, noticed that Holly Pointe was at last on the verge of springtime.

"It wasn't a fisher," she muttered under her breath.

"Oh?" Ned Granger's dull eyes grew even smaller. "If not a marten, then what?"

Milagros longed to tell someone of the burly faces in the fog, the call of her name. One look into Ned Granger's vacant eyes reminded her of the limitations of those who are terminally realistic.

"I'll be outside," she told John. It was a perfect chance to check on the damage to her dinghy. She scowled at Ned Granger on the way out toward the cliffs. "It *wasn't* fishers."

※ ※ ※

The cool breeze held the gulls aloft as they scavenged overhead. The water was blue glass, and seals were playing in the sparkly chop of the bay. Just as Patty had promised, lobster boats were back, and bright buoys bobbed in the distant waters to mark each man's traps. Soon the lobstermen would be making their way home in the afternoon to sell their catch and scrub down their boats for the night. Holly Pointe was not her home, but Milagros was surprised to find that it might have some beauty after all. She wondered if years from now she would remember this view fondly.

She inspected the dinghy, which John had kept near

the rocks. It had been scraped and dented, but he had been kind enough to patch its cracks. She ran her fingers over the warm wood and closed her eyes, hoping she might be able to find in her mind's eye the new place where she might go and belong. A sunny place, she hoped, one with palm trees whose fronds rustled in the late afternoon and whose polished sidewalks were always a bit gritty with white sand.

Mollie's whining soon interrupted her.

The dog was pawing the rocks and circling. Milagros checked her hind legs quickly. "What hurts?"

But Mollie was not in pain. She was wagging her tail, as was her habit when boats came close to the shoals. Milagros squinted into the bright light. No boats were nearby. Out among the seals, however, something extraordinary caught her eye. The water was becoming a kaleidoscope of color.

She held her breath and waited for a cloud to pass. She had to be sure it was not an odd reflection. Joy filled her. The water was alive with pulsating color. The rays had returned!

For a moment, she thought she should run and get Patty, who was far across the yard in her painting shed. She spied John in the window, still visiting with Ned Granger. Mollie whined and pawed the ground again; she sent out a long howl followed by three loud barks.

"Shhh. Stay quiet, dog," she ordered. The last thing she wanted was to get Ned Granger's attention. She rushed down the rocks alone to the water's edge and stood ankle-deep in the chilly water. She closed her eyes and concentrated. *Where are you?*

A small black object nearby bumped her foot. Looking down, she saw it was only a mermaid's purse, a pouch with pointed corners that looked like a tiny magic carpet cast out of the sea. She had seen these empty egg sacs often in Las Brisas. They belonged to sharks, usually; but skates left them behind, too. This was the first one—no, the only one—she had ever noticed in Holly Pointe. She reached for it.

Just then, a tiny ray swam from beneath it. It was the size of her finger, completely gray on top with white on its belly. The skate swam in a small circle, as if in a tornado of water. As she watched, its color began to change. Starting at the tail, it seemed to fill with colored ink until it was completely the rich purple of an eggplant. Too quickly, it turned back to gray.

The skate swam in another circle, and this time it became the color of a grapefruit's flesh. Milagros was fascinated and thrilled as it repeated its performance, each time taking on the color of a lime or a pink hibiscus and—once—even stripes.

Milagros let out a happy laugh. "I knew you'd come for me!"

Just then, an angry voice cut through the air.

"What are you doing there?"

Diana stood at the top of the cliff, hands on her hips, straining to see what held Milagros's attention at the water's edge.

Milagros thought desperately for a way to distract Diana. What had she seen? There was no telling what could happen if others knew about the rays, especially someone like Diana. They might try to capture the poor creatures and trap them in an aquarium where they would die.

She turned to the water.

"Gray," she ordered in a whisper. Instantly the skate faded to a putty color and darted off toward the deep.

"Nothing," Milagros called, forcing a smile. "Just looking at an empty mermaid's purse." She scrambled up the rock and forced herself to hold out the egg sac with the placid face of an angel. "It's good luck. You can have it."

Diana was not fooled. Resentment had sharpened her wits to points. She had arrived from school moments earlier and had already learned the terrible plan that Ned

Granger had hatched. She crossed her arms and eyed the mermaid's purse suspiciously.

"You're lying."

Milagros shrugged and tossed the sac far out toward the water. The iridescence had faded completely from view. *Get away from here,* Milagros thought, though she loved them dearly and wanted desperately to go with them. *Go far from this place before she finds you!* The idea of her precious rays being captured was even more heartbreaking than living out her days among pirate ghosts and jealous girls. She did not want to see them ruined. Captured, they would become so dull and unremarkable that they would never think themselves magical again.

She turned back to Diana, and in that single moment she bit from the same apple as Rosa had before her. The agony of sacrificing for another made her voice flat and distant.

"I'm not lying," she said. "I was watching the seals, and I found it." She walked slowly toward the house, her heart an anchor of remorse. She did not dare look back on all that she had let go.

Diana did not follow. She waited to hear the back door slam and then climbed down the rocks to inspect things herself. There was nothing but minnows in the water.

Disappointed, she sat down with a sigh. She was sure

she would find more answers this afternoon. After all, she had made a most curious find that morning at the water's edge, something that had distracted her in school as she plowed through her lessons. Rummaging in her leather sack, she pulled out the item. It had been glittering among the rocks.

Were you looking for this, Miracle?

In her hand, Diana held a red bottle, the glass etched with images of starfish all around the neck. At first, she had thought it was an ordinary bottle. People's silly wishes were always washing up on shore from other islands and the mainland.

But when she fished it from the chilly waters, she knew at once that it was something more. The bottle was as warm as her father's touch, as if it had been bobbing in a hot spring and not the cold northern sea. Uncorking it, she smelled its strange perfume.

She examined the bottle more closely now, so sure that she had found what belonged to Milagros. Still plugged inside was a slip of paper. Diana tipped it into her palm and read the Spanish words aloud.

Rosa vive.

Her agile mind followed tunnels, climbed ladders, and jumped hoops as it searched for an answer. Who was Rosa?

Someone important, no doubt. Someone Miracle

needed. Diana's mind jumped instantly to the person every girl needs to have for herself: her mother.

Could it be?

Next she studied the word *vive*. She knew enough to think of familiar words that sounded the same. *Vivid*: to be bright, colorful, just like her mother. But maybe, too, to be . . . *alive.*

Diana lay back and considered the information. What if Miracle's mother was alive?

The Winterses had been waiting for months for the girl's parents. This might be the solution to all Diana's problems. Rosa could be found and made to take her daughter away. Diana could have her family to herself once again.

But another darker possibility loomed.

What if Rosa was as destitute as her daughter? What if she was to join Miracle in Holly Pointe? Diana's parents would open their home to yet another stranger, just as they did for everyone in need, no matter how much they crowded out Diana.

She tucked the note back in the bottle and hid her treasure inside her sack before climbing back toward the house. She would not tell a soul what she had found. At least, not for now, not until she knew for certain what her parents would do.

After scaling the cliff, she rounded the house until

she came to the garden. There she spied the perfect hiding place. She buttoned the bottle inside the shirt pocket of the scarecrow that was leaning against the fence. No one would find it there.

"Come along, Mollie," she called sweetly as she entered the kitchen.

Milagros, she noted happily, was nowhere to be found.

CHAPTER 18

School Chums

Secrets never rest quietly, of course. They claw for their freedom, growing bitter in their unnatural solitude until they force someone to set them loose. Diana's secret was no different.

It tickled at the back of Milagros's neck when it came across the bluffs and wafted through her bedroom window at night. It giggled from behind the scraggly forsythias that blazed yellow near Patty's painting shed. It begged her again and again to come to the garden.

But Milagros foolishly turned a deaf ear. The garden, still barren after the harsh winter, reminded her of Rosa, and in her sadness about losing her rays, she told herself it was useless to dwell on the past. She turned to the two tasks at hand. As April gave way to May, Milagros roamed the island with Mollie, collecting sharp sticks and heavy stones (an odd habit, the islanders noted darkly). She was planning with great care how to guard herself and the Winterses from pirates.

And, of course, even more troubling was the looming matter of facing her first day of school.

John tooted his horn and waved eagerly from his truck. Milagros grabbed her empty book sack and tried her best to swat away memories of the last day she spent as a schoolgirl. It seemed so long ago.

Diana rounded the house from the garden and met her at the back door with a malicious smile. Milagros stopped and skewered Diana with a stare.

What are you hiding? she wanted to ask.

John leaned on the horn once again.

The trip down-island was quick. They bumped along in the truck and turned at a winding road that rose to a mossy hilltop. Diana said nothing the whole ride. She inched close to her father, irked by the merest touch of Milagros's leg inside the cramped cab.

Finally, Holly Pointe School came into view. It was nothing like Señorita Alma's elegant school, with its wrought-iron gates and captivating windows. This was an ordinary red barn, faded by saltwater and wind. It housed three classrooms for the island's twenty children, John explained. Everyone who lived in Holly Pointe studied here, preferring the safety of this modest building to a tiresome—and in winter, treacherous—ferry ride to the mainland to learn among Aways.

John sat inside his truck as the girls climbed out, the motor still idling. He leaned across the seat and spoke out the passenger window.

"Make sure Miracle gets to the upper-grade classroom, Diana," he said as he started to pull away. "And show her the way home in the afternoon."

"Okay, Daddy." When John had turned the corner, Diana whipped around to face Milagros. "Don't talk to me in there," she said. "You'll have to make your own friends." She ran off alone. Milagros was glad she had made careful mental notes of landmarks that would lead the way home later.

New children were unheard of in Holly Pointe, and everyone, even the adults, stopped to watch Milagros pass. She threw back her shoulders and walked inside slowly and deliberately, pretending the looks were of adulation, the way a queen's subjects gather to marvel at her glory as she passes.

The building was large and rustic, with a knotty-pine floor and a surprisingly pleasant scent of cedar.

Above were exposed wood rafters, and from these hung a papier-mâché testament to what these children knew of the world: moose, seals, lobsters, and scallop shells. Two walls were lined entirely with bookshelves, and they were filled, top to bottom, with more shiny-spine volumes than Milagros had ever seen in all of Las Brisas. When friendships failed, as she knew they would, she would find comfort inside the pages of these books.

Then, something unusual caught her eye. At the center of the open space was an old ship's bell—as tall as a young child—mounted on an arch. Its bronze was nearly black with age, and it was craggy and dented. Milagros made her way toward it, curious about its presence and about the words on the brass plate at its base. She read the words quietly: THE *ANNA MAY*. NINETEENTH OF MARCH 1863. NO SURVIVORS.

"It's all that was left after she sank," a voice said.

Milagros turned to find a girl about her age. She was pale and wore her light brown hair in a bun. The girl tapped the plaque.

"She shipwrecked on our shoals," she said, not bothering with introductions. "Fog, of course." She nudged Milagros, reached inside the bell, and sighed. "Move over, please. It's time."

The girl rang the clapper five times. Each clang reverberated through the barn in a deafening peal. Milagros was sure it could be heard up-island in the Winterses' kitchen, out in the farthest reaches of the harbor, down at the bottom of the sea where the pirates' bones lay sleeping. It was an astonishing sound, ageless and powerful. She remembered at once her grandfather's book of sea lore. Bells like this sent warnings to passing ships hidden in the fog. She felt her hands grow moist as she imagined its frantic clangs on the night the *Anna May* had sunk amid the voices of pirates cackling at the ship's demise.

Milagros shook her head to clear the dreary thought. Older students scampered up wooden steps that were nearly as steep as the rungs of a ladder to what had once been the loft. Younger students, Diana among them, disappeared inside the two classrooms on the first floor. In a moment, the girl had vanished, the halls were abandoned, and the only sound was the click of each classroom door closing.

She was late.

Milagros rushed up the steps to the loft. At the landing were three lunch tables and empty stools all around. A door was at the far end. Carefully, she opened it and stepped inside.

She had not completely turned around when she heard a sharp and familiar voice call out.

"You've decided to join us."

Mrs. Mulligan, Ned Granger's friend, stood at the

back of the room. She wore a crooked little smile, and her pale arms were crossed at her chest. Her glasses were balanced on the tip of her nose.

"We've been expecting you, Miracle," she said grandly, "although by my watch at least four minutes ago."

She turned to the students, who were still staring at Milagros. "I'm sure you've heard of the Girl from Away. She is staying with the Winters family for a time, until her *real* family is found. She calls herself Miracle."

At this, she locked her eyes on Milagros and smiled to reveal her small yellow teeth. Mrs. Mulligan lumbered along the few desks toward the front of the room as she spoke. "Sit here, next to Sara," she said, pointing to an empty seat beside the girl who had rung the bell. She looked once again at the class. "Please speak slowly and be kind."

Milagros felt her cheeks blaze as all eyes followed her. She cleared her throat and tried to stand tall.

"No one has to speak slowly. I understand you perfectly."

The children watched their teacher's face nervously. Mrs. Mulligan arched her brow.

"What a *charming* way of speaking," she said, but it still sounded like an insult. "Away accents are so sweet and curious. Sweet as *sugar*, in fact."

Milagros stared straight ahead, fuming. She would have given anything to see Señorita Alma's face at that moment! She couldn't remember a single time that she had ever felt disliked or shamed by her old teacher, even after she had pulled her trickiest prank. Milagros found her way to the spot Mrs. Mulligan had indicated. Things would be different now. She could read Mrs. Mulligan's heart easily. This was a woman who sniffed for the failures of others.

As Mrs. Mulligan turned away, a voice mumbled near Milagros's ear.

"Old witch."

Milagros was sure it was Sara, but when she turned, the girl's face was a blank slate bent over the first of a long list of mathematics problems. Sara gave a sideways glance and then, so fleetingly Milagros thought she had imagined it, she smiled.

Milagros studied her teacher carefully before turning to her work.

Once Eugenia had scratched *witch* in the dirt entrance of Rosa's market stall. The letters had vanished under her mother's feet as she crossed the threshold, laughing.

Mildred Mulligan, a witch? Not a chance, she told herself firmly.

At noon Milagros found her way to a window seat in

the loft that overlooked the grass where most of the younger students played. The midday sun had chased away the damp and now the day was clear. She pulled out the sandwich that John had prepared for her that morning and sat in a slant of sunshine. Sara soon joined her.

Sara was only a bit older, perhaps a year or two, Milagros judged from the corner of her eye. She also had an intelligent face and wasted no time on small talk.

"I've heard say you're a runaway from a family that hated you and beat you bloody," she said in between bites of her sandwich. "Is it true?"

"No."

"Oh," Sara said, obviously disappointed.

"Is that why you all stare at me? If it is, you're silly."

"It's not only that," Sara answered matter-of-factly. "You're an Away." She curled her nose and took a sip of her drink. "Why should we trust you?"

Milagros chewed silently. She thought of how foolishly her neighbors had trusted the Rubians—and how high a price they had all paid. She couldn't begrudge Sara her suspicions. At least it proved she wasn't stupid.

"Maybe you shouldn't," Milagros said.

Sara arched her brow and smiled again. Then she looked down at the field and brightened. She pointed at someone else, a redheaded boy with prominent teeth playing baseball. "That's Fang. I might love him. What do you think?"

Delfín's teeth sparkled before Milagros's eyes. "Don't trust him," she said.

Sara considered the advice. "Hmmm," she said. "You could be right."

They finished their lunch in companionable silence until the bell pealed once again, though this time, urgently. A girl in pigtails and a devilish grin rang it as though a fire were spreading. Students everywhere were holding their ears in pain, and the vibrations were making the windowpanes in the loft rattle. Sara ran to the railing.

"Quit that, Eloise!" she shouted. She turned to Milagros and rolled her eyes. "My sister."

They watched as Eloise, no more than eight, ducked inside her classroom before any adult could spot her. Diana came running across the room below.

"It was Eloise!" Diana told her teacher. She was pointing. "I saw her, Mrs. Pennington. It was Eloise."

"Snitch," Sara growled down. She put her hands on her hips. "What's it like living with that one?" she asked, motioning at Diana.

Milagros felt her tongue thicken. *It's horrible. She's a hateful beast. I loathe her*, she was about to say. She bit her tongue instead and shrugged.

Sara gathered her trash and nodded knowingly. "I thought so. *You're* not a snitch, are you?"

Milagros did not have time to reply. Classmates had begun to clamor up the steps to face the drudgery of the afternoon. She studied the ship's bell once again before following the others to their room. Its last echoes of warning were finally fading. Again, she felt the presence of a secret that was just out of her reach.

"You're planning to be late again, are you?"

Mrs. Mulligan's hand rested firmly on her shoulder. The old woman was red-faced and out of breath from the steep climb. Cold suspicion filled her eyes.

Milagros ducked out of her bony hands. "No, Señora Mulligan," she said as she hurried into the room.

CHAPTER 19

Regrets

Rosa sat surrounded by a pile of dirty boots, each waiting to be shined. She slid her arm into a boot as though it were an evening glove and rubbed vigorously. At her current speed, she would be shining boots until nightfall.

Her mind roamed as she worked. If they never laid eyes on each other again, what would Milagros remember of her? Rosa wondered. What would *she* remember of her daughter when she was old and feeble . . . if she reached old age at all?

She considered this carefully as she scrubbed sea salt from a brass buckle. She was certain it would be the tiny memories: the pattern of sun and shade on her daughter's baby blanket; finding Milagros asleep in her bed, her dusty feet poking from the bottom of the sheet; the curl of Milagros's eyelashes as she read from her schoolbooks. The moments—all unnoticed scraps, now suddenly priceless.

Rosa picked caked mud from the sole of another boot. She had squandered precious time with her daughter by working long hours in the field. And now there was no use even asking the question or having regrets. Time for Milagros and Rosa had stopped. There was no chance of making more happy days together. She would have to content herself with the job she had done, for better or worse. Rosa brushed the boot in her hand violently.

Maybe Milagros would forget her altogether? It could be better, less confusing. Rosa closed her eyes. She sighed deeply, her sorrow—so unknown to her until now— circling the *Ruby Sails* before dissipating into the still air.

Far away on the shore, an old woman sat in the shade of a palm tree at noon, a fat infant wailing in her arms. These afternoons in the Yucatán sun were far too torrid for her after so many years away. Her skin was no longer accustomed to the searing heat of May, never mind how uncomfortable it must be for a baby's new skin. She looked back toward the small wooden house facing the beach and saw her daughter, Mercedes, at the sink preparing cold drinks. She had grown up beautifully after all. *Well, at least I am alive to see it*, thought the woman.

"Too hot, yes?" she said to the baby. She pulled his tiny undershirt over his head and blew gently on his tender brown skin. He was a spectacular one, this boy. A head full of black hair and big, curious eyes, deep and dark enough to hold all the knowledge of the world. He would be like his grandfather: strong, though hopefully luckier.

She kissed the baby's wet forehead and tickled her index finger against his mouth. He took it eagerly. This would do for a few minutes until his mother could feed him. The tiniest breeze crossed the woman's face. She was surprised to feel a faint squeeze in her chest. Not the squeeze of an old heart announcing its trouble. It was something else entirely, and she knew it well. It made her shudder.

She peered out at the water and walked to its edge, though she did not venture in. Sea snakes, *tiburones* like the terrible bull sharks, all manner of angry biting crustaceans lurked in the water.

Again the wind rippled through her hair and she felt the same sensation. Still, she saw nothing. Her old eyes, of course, could not see the *Ruby Sails* haunting the waters so many miles away. She certainly could not hear the mumbled prayers of its broken prisoner. She had never met a girl named Milagros.

But she knew this familiar tightness in her chest. It was the burning of an old sorrow among women. It was the sad tale of all mothers and children who have lost each other. It was the terrible squeeze of longing and regret.

The old woman rose and, with the baby, hurried back toward the house.

CHAPTER 20

Gardening

Milagros took a deep breath of the damp morning air as she finished making her complaint to John. They were in the garden, doing the spring planting now that at long last the danger of frost had passed. Though it was the middle of May, the air was still cooled by the ocean, and mornings were chilly. Together they had weeded and tilled the rows until their fingernails were filled with black crescents of dirt and their hair smelled of dew. John had put a new hat on the scarecrow and bought plants from the Sally Stevens seed catalog. Milagros walked through the soft mud behind him, a marvelous peace filling her. She had never liked to work the rows of her mother's groves, yet something in John's garden felt natural and safe. It calmed her completely and coaxed her to air out her tired thoughts in the breeze.

"I am counting the days until the end of June." And she was, one by one, in pencil on the wall by her bed. Only thirty-two school days remained.

John shook his head and smiled wistfully as she continued to explain about her dreary days in Mrs. Mulligan's care. The ugly glances and the suspicious looks when Milagros's work was excellent. The delight she took in correcting the students' smallest mistakes in her very loudest voice. How she had given Milagros the oldest books whose pages were dog-eared and covers stained.

"Oh, Mildred Mulligan . . . she's been the same since I was a boy," John assured Milagros as he patted the small tomato plants into the soil. The summer festival would be upon them soon. It began the first weekend of July with the arrival of carnival rides and artisans, and it lasted the whole summer long. He had no time to lose in preparing for its many competitions, including the annual tomato contest. Other islanders were already adding sulphur to their blueberry beds to encourage the best harvest for their pies in August. They were boasting of chowder recipes and adding bonemeal to their prize-winning rugosa roses. They were, as John and Milagros would be that afternoon, shoveling chicken manure into their vegetable gardens and hoping against any late frosts or drought.

Milagros tried to imagine John as a child. It was easy. His eyes still had the wonder that some adults can hold on to. But Mrs. Mulligan young and smooth? Impossible! "I hope she liked you. She hates me."

John stretched his back and surveyed the row, noticing that Milagros had already set five or six more plants than he had.

"Hates you? I doubt it. But it's true she's difficult. Angry." He looked at the puzzled look on Milagros's face. "Pastor Mulligan, her husband, was still alive when I was in school. He died a few years ago. Left a big hole for Mrs. Mulligan, the way it does when you lose people you love. That's what's made her bitter."

Milagros remained silent, her fingers moving expertly as she tied the tender shoots to the stakes. It was hard to imagine Mrs. Mulligan loving anyone.

John cleared his throat. "Pastor Mulligan, now, that was a good man. I owe that man a huge debt."

"He was rich?" Milagros asked.

"No, no. Not that kind of debt. I mean, he did something that I can never repay. It's because of him that I'm here today. He's why I'm alive at all."

He drove his shovel deep into the soil and stole a glance at Milagros, who was waiting expectantly. Then, he pointed out toward the water. "I grew up on the mainland at the Newton Home for Boys. Most people don't hold it in account, since it's the pastor who brought me to Holly Pointe later." He lowered his voice. "I never met my parents. I was abandoned near the pier. I'm told it was just a few days after I was born. I was nearly frozen—all blue, covered in filth, and tossed among rusted traps. Pastor Mulligan had come in on his skiff, the *Miracle*, when he found me."

"Your parents threw you away?"

John gave an uncomfortable snort. "Hard to imagine someone just tossing away a child, isn't it? To this day, no one knows who my parents were or why they chose to do something so reckless. For all I know, they're dead."

Milagros put down her spade and studied the lines etched around John's eyes. She had sensed his sadness the first time they met. Now she understood.

"Do you hate them?" she asked boldly.

The question hung in the air for a long time. John looked out over the water, thinking. "I do not. Not anymore. I didn't know them. What I've settled on is that I just don't understand what they did."

"I would hate them," she said.

"Oh, I did for a long, long while, and it made me miserable. But an islander learns that life is equal parts joy to hardship. It's the hard times that teach us. It might have been to my advantage to be raised without them. It might be a good thing to have been thrown away, after all. They certainly didn't have any good sense. They might have been heartless, or maybe they just didn't know any better, or I don't know what. But I got too tired of being angry and hating them. Forgiveness is what Pastor Mulligan liked to call it. Can't say I think of it as forgiveness exactly, even today. He'd feel sad about that. But the important thing is that I took the sadness out of my story. That's relief, I can tell you. I can finally say out loud, *I was left in the trash,* and it doesn't make me want to hurt anybody the way it once did."

He finished his row and moved on. When Milagros didn't answer, he broke into a nervous smile and said a little too brightly, "And now, I have a good life. A warm house, fruitful garden, enough to do. I met Patty; we've got Diana." He paused. "And now you."

John surveyed her progress. "You're good with these plants. Those peppers you planted last week have shot up at least twice the size of the ones I put in," he said, pointing to the lush corner of the patch. "You have a green thumb. You must have had some practice back home."

Milagros shrugged. "My mother was a gardener." It was the first time she had mentioned Rosa directly. The word *mother* felt dry in her mouth.

"Is that right?" John said as he pushed three stakes into the loose soil. Milagros could not tell if he really believed that there was such a place, or if, like Mrs. Mulligan, he thought she had made the whole story up.

"Yes, on Las Brisas," she said a bit tersely. "She was called Rosa, and she was a farmer. We had groves that gave the best fruit."

"Well, Rosa must have been a very good farmer, because you are a natural."

Milagros swallowed hard. "Yes. She was good."

"And your father?" he asked carefully. "Did he plant things, too?"

Milagros thought about this for a moment. The whole story seemed too ugly to share, and she hardly knew where to begin. Still, John had just shared his own story. She couldn't be aloof now. "Only trouble," Milagros said at last. "He left. He was a pirate"—and then, in case he didn't believe her, she added quickly, "a real pirate."

John stopped his work and glued his eyes on the hole he was digging with a spade. "So what about you, Miracle? Do you hate your parents?"

The question felt like a sledgehammer shattering her darkest and most private feelings. Why did he want her to talk about such things? Even if she were thinking these things, wasn't she justified? Parents were supposed to care for their children. And what had hers done? Nothing of the kind.

Milagros's eyes grew cloudy. She wanted to say yes, she hated them for not protecting her. She even wanted to say she hated John for asking. But instead she heard herself say the truth that kept her awake so many nights. "I loved my parents very much. I was a good girl for them. But they did not love me the same way. Maybe I was too much trouble. Maybe it was too hard to love me."

John collected the discarded trays of tomato plants and politely ignored Milagros's quivering lip and the tears swimming in her eyes.

"Sometimes parents don't love their children. Not often, but it can happen. Sometimes they can't love them because they don't know how. Or else they love them the best that they can, and it's still not enough. Maybe it was one of those ways with your parents."

Milagros ran her hand across her face and took a deep breath. "My father loved his own adventure more than he loved me. That is simple to see. And my mother . . . she couldn't have loved me very much. She sent me here alone to this cold place where I am just the Girl from Away. I am like one of your cats in the yard. I have no people of my own, no family or friends. No one here knows my language or my games, the way I swam or climbed trees.

It is like I began only when I came off the boat. There is not even a food that tastes like what I know. I hate being here alone. It is a mother with no love that would do such a bad thing to me."

She felt her face burning as John came toward her. *Why aren't you my father?* she thought.

John put one arm around her gently, noticing for a moment that she had grown at least two inches taller just since she'd arrived that winter. Soon she would stop looking like a little girl, her body catching up to all of her experiences.

"You are right to be sad," he said simply. "It's lonely to be in a place that is so different from home with no one who seems like you at the moment."

Milagros could feel her voice rising in frustration. "My parents did this to me. It's their fault. They threw me away, John, like your parents. They are never coming for me."

Shame and frustration filled Milagros as she began to sob for the first time in Holly Pointe. In her mind's eye, she could see her mother's face the way she never wanted to remember it. Rosa dragged down to the sand by her attacker, begging her daughter to run. She knew that her mother had saved her life, but suffering ate at any gratitude until all that was left was a bone of resentment.

"I miss her. I miss my mother so much. I hate her for leaving me alone."

John found no words as she cried. His heart raced the way it had when he was a boy, orphaned and loose in the world.

He watched as her tears fell inside the porous earth beneath them both. Silenced, all he could offer was to hold her hand.

CHAPTER 21

The Wife Discovered

The sun was orange fire in the sky as the *Ruby Sails* rocked gently on the calm sea. The ship's lookout, perched in the crow's nest for hours, stared out blankly at the empty horizon, his eyelids heavy with sleep. He was alone on his watch, except for Rosa, hungry and thirsty on the deck below. His fellow pirates had sought shade in their quarters long ago.

The blistering sun had beaten down on Rosa all morning. Her head burned, her arms felt prickly, and her legs were unsteady. She stared longingly at the keys around the lookout's waist, one of which could surely open her shackles.

Rosa closed her eyes and tried to concentrate on a tiny breeze that fluttered across the deck. With food and water growing scarce, the lookout would offer her a biscuit and refill her water jug only once in a day's time.

But not even her terrible thirst and hunger could compare to her yearning for Milagros. Again, she gazed up at the key on the lookout's waist, her possible escape. Rosa could call to him and claim illness. Or beg him—even threaten him—with the pick she used for cleaning boots. She closed her dry eyes again and leaned back against the mast. Strength had abandoned her. Even begging was too difficult now.

As the hours ticked by, Rosa began to work less and less. She closed her eyes and tried to summon the mantas, to no avail. Finally, without the slightest alarm, she slipped into waking dreams of Las Brisas, where she heard the murmur of women at her stall on market day and the squeak of her wagon's wheels, heavy under the weight of avocadoes and flowers.

"*Que Dios te bendiga,*" a voice whispered clearly in her ear. Rosa turned. Silhouetted against the bright sun was a familiar stooped shape of an old man. It was the blind street sweeper, *el viejo* José. He was forming the sign of the cross over her with his gnarled hands.

"I have no tea or liniment, old friend," she said sadly. She did not have the heart to tell him that he could not clean Avenida Central. She could not tell him that everything that mattered to them both was gone.

"You will rest now," he said, patting her gently as he lowered himself next to her.

She leaned her head toward the old man's bony shoulder, only to find the hard mast once again. Her friend had vanished.

What was that sound? Rosa listened carefully. *Is that you, Milagros?* The girl's voice seemed to rise from the very floorboards. Rosa put her ear down against the warm wood to listen. Yes, there it was: Milagros playing happily with Miguel. She let the music of her daughter's voice fill her heart.

"Wake up, woman!"

The familiar gruff voice startled Rosa.

"Miguel?" she answered. Had she fallen asleep? Impossible! And yet, as she struggled to her knees, she found that night had, indeed, fallen. The sky above was a dark blanket dotted with white stars.

She drank greedily from the jug of water he held out to her.

"Where is she, husband? I heard her voice. Where have you hidden her, Miguel?"

She was yanked suddenly to her feet. Rosa could feel sour breath cover her face as an iron grip closed around her wrists. Fully awake, she could now see it was not Miguel at all. Instead, the sunburned lookout smiled a toothless grin.

"Husband, you say? Miguel is your husband?" His hot breath filled her face. "El Capitán will want to know about this."

He dragged the delirious Rosa to the captain's quarters below.

CHAPTER 22

The Return of
Old Woman Pérez

What is asleep in the roots will flower in its time. It is true of plants, and it is true of people.

Like Rosa, Milagros was an enchantress with nature. After her talk with John, she began to listen to the call of the garden. Sometimes she worked alongside him in the weak sunshine of dawn; other times she preferred to dig, water, and prune on her own. She spent happy hours in that way, especially after school, when Diana's presence crowded the house. The garden was safe and inviting, as though it wanted Milagros to tend it. She donned a baggy pair of shorts and John's old boots to clomp along the rows. She pinched off shriveled marigold leaves and marveled at the smell of rain, the undulations of snails, and spiderwebs coated in silvery dew when the last of the fog pulled away. She now understood how Rosa must have loved all these things and wondered why she had never spoken of them.

One Friday afternoon, Milagros walked the rows pondering John's pepper plants, unacceptably puny three weeks after their planting. She scolded them like a schoolmistress. "*Vamos, ajíes.* You have everything you need. No need to be stingy." Rosa had always talked to plants as though they were people. "Everything has a soul and a heart that can be coaxed," she'd say. Thinking about her now, Milagros recalled her mother's voice exactly. The sound was so clear that she stopped her work, closed her eyes, and cocked her head into the breeze. "Mamá?" she said aloud. No response; just the scarecrow shifting slightly in the wind.

It was when she straightened herself and opened her eyes again that Milagros first laid eyes on Old Woman Pérez.

Milagros watched the approaching figure, feeling frozen, as though she were seeing a ghost. The woman was leaning heavily into her cane as she worked her way up the drive, a brown package wrapped in string under her arm. Mollie raced alongside barking, but the woman seemed unperturbed. She had leathery, coffee-colored skin and thick white hair pulled into a bun at the back of her neck. Her white gauze blouse was decorated with embroidery around its square collar, and her loose skirt flapped in the breeze. Milagros held her breath. Was this a mirage? This old woman could pass for any of the *abuelitas* who lived on Las Brisas. *¡Pan y mantequilla!*— fresh bread and butter for sale, they would call as she passed them on her way to school.

Milagros rinsed her hands quickly under the spigot, dried them on her jeans, and peeked carefully around the side of the house.

The woman was out of breath by the time she had reached the top of the hill. She hooked her cane over the gate, ambled the remaining few steps to the front door, and knocked. In a few moments, Patty appeared, smiling.

"I wasn't expecting you, Elvirita! Welcome home!"

The woman bowed her head and offered the package marked DAY'S MENDING.

"*Para la niña Diana,*" she said in perfect Spanish that hypnotized Milagros at once. Then, in heavily accented English, she continued, "The hems are all done on the summer pants. Also the zipper on the white ones looked bad, so I changed it. Miss Diana is looking forward to a long summer this year? Yes?"

Patty lowered her voice. "It's been a difficult time for her," she said carefully. "But all children look forward to summer, don't they?"

"Of course," the woman replied.

Patty took the package. "You shouldn't have walked all this way. I would have been happy to send Diana along for them."

But the woman raised her hand and shook her head. "It is nothing on a pleasant day. This kind weather is so short here that it is a shame not to enjoy it. And Dr. Hughes says my old knee needs to stay in practice." The woman glanced toward the garden; Milagros moved back out of view.

"Well, in that case, thank you so much for bringing them by. It's saved me a trip," said Patty. "But please come in. I'd love for you to meet someone. You've heard about our wonderful houseguest? She arrived while you were visiting your daughter."

Milagros held her breath.

"I have heard the happy news. But I am so sorry. I cannot stay today. I am needed at the shop."

Patty's voice was disappointed. "Another time?"

"Of course! We will find a day when it is not so busy for Mr. Day. Good-bye, Mrs. Winters."

Milagros heard the front door close and the shuffle of the old woman's shoes dragging toward the road. She waited for a few moments and, hearing no more noise, stepped out to watch her go. How shocking to find the old woman standing motionless and staring straight at her from the fence.

"That is a good garden," she said in Spanish. Her keen eyes surveyed the rows and fell at last on the scarecrow. Then she reached into her pocket and drew out a small white card. She lifted it in the air and placed it carefully on the crossbeam of the fence. She bowed her head slightly. Grasping her cane, she called over her shoulder, "*Adiós.*"

Milagros edged out from behind the house and reached the gate. A small business card lay on top. It read: DAY'S MENDING, HOLLY POINTE PIER. It was followed by the phone number and address.

When she looked up, the woman was gone.

Chapter 23

Cafecito

The following day, Milagros stood under a large lamppost at the pier. She had finished her gardening by seven that morning and had headed alone to the town square. She had brought with her a pair of old pants from Sara. Milagros, having grown taller, as she always did in spring, now owned only pants that left her ankles exposed. She didn't care, of course, about her appearance, even if her classmates smirked, but the pants provided a handy excuse for a visit to the seamstress about whom she had been thinking all night.

When she reached the shop, she was disappointed to find it dark inside, the Closed sign turned outward, the cast-iron sewing machine in the window abandoned. The shop would not open until ten. With more than an hour and a half to spare, she wandered toward the pilings, feeling foolish for having come at all.

She thought of all Patty had told her at dinner. Everyone called the island's seamstress Old Woman Pérez, and though she was once from Away, she had been in Holly Pointe so long that people finally considered her an islander. She lived alone, above the tailor-and-mend shop.

"She's very private," Patty had told her as she hung wind chimes outside the kitchen window that morning. "I was so shocked to see her at our front door, but then, Elvirita Pérez has always struck me as a bit of a surprise. You might enjoy meeting her, Miracle. She is from somewhere in Mexico, I think."

Milagros sat at the edge of the pier to wait. The warmer weather had lured the island's residents from their winter hibernation. Shops would soon latch open their screen doors for the day, an invitation for shoppers to congregate on the porches to predict the weather or report on squabbles with their more cantankerous neighbors.

A tapping drew Milagros's attention to the windows above the dark shop. There she saw Old Woman Pérez standing by the curtains, motioning in her direction.

"That way," she called through the closed glass, pointing with her cane toward the side of the building.

Milagros hesitated for a moment and then crossed

the street. Feral cats crouched low on the cover of a trash can and stared in surprise, flat-eared, as Milagros approached. They lunged off their perch and scattered into the empty street.

Old Woman Pérez leaned over the stair railing. She wore another embroidered dress that revealed knee-high stockings before Milagros could look away. The wood stairs were buckled in spots, a bit wobbly as well, but not exactly dangerous. Still, how a woman with a bad leg could navigate them was another matter.

By the time Milagros reached the open door at the top of the stairs, Old Woman Pérez had disappeared inside the apartment.

"*Adelante, adelante,*" called the woman. Come in, come in.

Milagros stepped inside and was welcomed by the smell of black coffee percolating on the stove. It was the very smell that had greeted her every morning of her life in Las Brisas.

The room had dark wood floors and two large windows that faced the pier and ocean. On the far wall was a narrow sink with two small cupboards above. Old Woman Pérez leaned inside a refrigerator that was no taller than Milagros. Elsewhere the furnishings were as sparse as those of a nun's room: a twin-sized bed (made neatly in sheets only) and a small round table and two wooden chairs. The rest of the room was dominated by cardboard boxes brimming with spools of thread, balls of yarn, scissors, pincushions, marking chalk, and what seemed like millions of scraps of fabrics.

"*Cafecito* with our breakfast," Old Woman Pérez announced—a statement, not an offer—as she pulled out a can of evaporated milk and turned to the stove to turn off the flame. In a moment, she placed a steaming cup of coffee in front of Milagros. Light with milk and very sweet, Milagros noticed as she took her first eager sip. Old Woman Pérez eased herself down and held her bad leg straight as a plank. She looked carefully at Milagros as she drank her own coffee in silence. After several minutes, she folded her hands, smiled primly, and then spoke in Spanish.

"Mr. Day sent word to me many weeks ago that you had arrived. Please accept my apologies that I could not come immediately. First, there is the matter of the winter here, which by now you know is demonic. But more important, I was visiting my daughter in Mexico." She smiled, and Milagros stared at her mouth: pretty teeth, small and white, one gold at the back. The sound of her voice was music. "How nice that we can meet at last."

Milagros felt her cheeks flush with excitement. To keep Old Woman Pérez talking, she slid the pants across the table. "I've brought pants to be fixed," she mumbled.

"Oh, yes?" she said without looking at them. "Well, in any case, I'm sorry I was not here when you arrived. Helping strangers is what we learned in my hometown. It was this way in Las Brisas, I assume. It couldn't be helped this time, however. Mercedes was having a baby, my grandson, Héctor. I am an *abuelita* now. It is a very happy occasion for me."

"Congratulations," Milagros offered.

"Thank you." She reached inside the top of her dress and pulled out a small, worn picture that was tucked under the strap of her brassiere. "He is lovely, is he not?"

Milagros looked at the picture of the round-faced, black-haired baby, his eyes two swollen slits in his smooth face. "Yes. Lovely," she lied.

Old Woman Pérez took back the picture, smiled as she looked at her grandson once more and tucked it back inside her undergarment. "So, let us start properly, yes? I'll begin. I am Señora Elvirita Pérez, wife of the late Sergio Guitiérrez of the town of Mar Azul in Mexico."

Milagros nodded, but Old Woman Pérez seemed to be waiting for a reply.

"I suppose you have a name and a family somewhere, yes? You can explain why you are here alone?" she coaxed.

Remembering her Brisenian manners, Milagros cleared her throat.

"I am Milagros de la Torre," she began quietly. "I am from Las Brisas, a small island in the Caribbean sea—"

"A fine people, the Brisenians," Old Woman Pérez interjected.

Milagros stopped. "You know of Las Brisas?"

"Of course. The 'jewel of the Caribbean' is what I've always heard. My husband, Sergio, lived there as a boy, I think. That was many years ago, long before I met him. I don't know anyone from there now. Except, of course, you."

Milagros felt more comfortable. "I am Milagros, the daughter of Rosa de Santiago and Miguel de la Torre." She lowered her eyes. "Rosa is—was—a farmer, killed in an attack. Miguel is nothing more than a shameless pirate. You have heard correctly, *señora*. I am here alone."

Old Woman Pérez narrowed her eyes and leaned forward. She pulled Milagros's face into her own, studying every inch of Milagros's skin as though searching for a secret. Embarrassed, Milagros focused on the embroidery around Old Woman Pérez's collar while she was being examined. From this close angle, the bright threads were winged splotches all connected with a coiling green thread. She held her breath until Old Woman Pérez released her.

"Yes, of course, that's true. It's right there in your face."

"What is?" Milagros touched her hands to her own cheeks.

Old Woman Pérez chuckled softly. "Your life story. All this worry these sweet northern people have of how to find the truth," she said, clicking her tongue. "I imagine some might not believe you? I hope you haven't had to tangle too much with Officer Granger. Perhaps his pants are too tight? He should come into the shop so I can fix them," she said mischievously. Milagros let a tiny laugh escape.

"The answer to their question is right here, of course," Old Woman Pérez said. "The map of your town is right here."

Milagros pulled away sharply. "Map?" The Rubians' map had changed her fate completely.

Old Woman Pérez nodded and placed her hands on Milagros's face. "Can you feel it?" She ran her thumb gently across Milagros's forehead and then into her black hair. Milagros felt her skin turn to gooseflesh.

"Your parents," she said more softly, "are here." She

ran her fingers from the outer edge of Milagros's eyes down to the corner of her mouth and then said earnestly, "You say your mother is dead?"

Milagros nodded.

Old Woman Pérez moved her fingers along Milagros's cheeks again and knotted her brow in confusion. Finally, she said, "Well, I am sorry she is not with you now."

Milagros closed her eyes as Old Woman Pérez continued. With both index fingers she continued tracing two lines from the corners of Milagros's mouth down to her jaw. "And here is now, with the Winters family in Holly Pointe. A little harsh, but a fine new home—"

"No. This will never feel like my home," she answered quickly. She was herself shutting the opening to her private story. But Old Woman Pérez jammed her foot discreetly in that door and pressed on.

"Oh, no? You want to leave?" she observed politely. "But please tell me, are you not feeling welcome here on our island? Mr. and Mrs. Winters have been unkind?"

"It's not that." She looked out the window, thinking of the dangerous mists, of Diana's bitterness. "I just don't belong here."

Old Woman Pérez leaned forward and narrowed her eyes. "Where do you belong then, if not where life has brought you?"

Milagros pretended to take a long sip from her nearly empty cup.

Old Woman Pérez softened her features once again. "Ah, well, there's no need to wet your feet before you've reached the river. There's plenty of time to face the future, plenty of time." She put her hand to her forehead and seemed to remember something suddenly. "Oh, how rude of me! Here, I have something you might like. Not as good as back in Las Brisas, but not bad this far away." She reached for a small wax paper package and extended it to Milagros.

Inside was Milagros's favorite treat: *queso con guayaba*—sticky squares of guava paste placed neatly on slices of white cheese. In spite of herself, Milagros broke into a smile and popped a fruit and cheese slice into her mouth greedily. The salty cheese and the sweetness of the guava melted on her tongue.

"I have always loved the salt and sweet together," Old Woman Pérez began as though she were reading Milagros's mind. "Some might think these two things are so different and so should not be together. But for my tongue, it's always an unusual surprise. I love a good surprise, don't you?"

Old Woman Pérez proceeded to ask a million questions that morning with no worry of prying. With a full stomach and sticky fingers, Milagros felt the warm glow of comfort rising from within, and it made her grow bolder as they spoke. The seamstress nodded in concentration as she listened to Milagros's adventure, holding her heart and proclaiming "Barbarians!" at all the appropriate times. She smiled to hear of Patty's painting and grew thoughtful at stories of Diana's hateful words. Finally, Milagros confessed the disquieting details of Mollie's attack.

"There are spirits here, *señora*," she whispered. "Pirates. They've followed me."

Old Woman Pérez remained the picture of serenity. "Everyone's past has a few unhappy ghosts, I suppose. Mine certainly does. Such pests! They don't want to rest until everyone is as miserable as they are. Thank goodness, you look strong enough to battle them."

Not since her days with Señorita Alma had Milagros felt so comfortable and understood. It was wonderful to simply let her tongue roll in her own language and not have to explain how things were in her old place or prove that she was anything at all.

Finally, with the last morsels of *queso con guayaba* gone, it was Milagros's turn to ask questions.

"Sergio and I had only short years together," Old Woman Pérez explained when Milagros wanted to know how she had come to Holly Pointe. "He was a good man, a good worker, though sometimes a drinker, it's true. He died when his voice was still strong, his hair black, and his body like an ox—right at our bedside. And what felled such a man in only two days' time? A tiny scorpion curled in his boot. A little thing, harmless until its time, angry to be disturbed. And so without warning, I found myself penniless with a baby girl to feed. A mountain of sorrows."

"That's terrible," said Milagros sympathetically.

Old Woman Pérez waved her hand. "Perhaps . . . but who had time to think of that? Such thoughts are a luxury when one is truly in trouble. You are learning that now, *mi hija*. And if not, you will do well to know. Self-pity is useless. No, I had to think fast and feed us both. What job was there for a young woman with almost no schooling and a wailing baby on her hip? No job at all. Or at least not one that could feed us for more than a few days at a time. At last, when my stomach was wrung like a washrag, I had no choice but to talk to my aunt Carmen. She lived in the city and had room for my girl, but only if I could give her some money. She had expenses for her hair and her clothing and such. That Carmen, she was no fool. She had always liked the good life, and *that* life costs money. So I was back to the same problem, yes?

Needing money and having none. How would you have solved my problem, Milagros?"

Milagros thought for a moment about a woman living in the days when Old Woman Pérez would have been young. Those were the silly days when women needed men to protect them. "Maybe marry another man? Is that what you did?"

"Another man! *¡Dios mío!* What a horror! Do I look foolish to you? Another man, another set of worries. No. I gave up. I resolved to starve. It actually seemed easier."

"But you didn't starve," pointed out Milagros. "You're here, and now you're a grandmother. You found Holly Pointe."

Old Woman Pérez gave a deep laugh. "You're right. I did not starve, even though I had truly decided to do so. I found Holly Pointe the way all of us find the true place we belong. Despite ourselves. Do you know Mr. Day? The owner of the shop downstairs? Back then, Mr. Day was something of an adventurer, especially for a man born and raised in a place like Holly Pointe. He was honeymooning in a hotel in Mar Azul, the very hotel with a grand front sidewalk where I had decided to sell the last of my embroidery. His wife had fallen in love with Mar Azul, and she wanted one of my blouses, the one with big sleeves and a string of butterflies at each cuff to remind her of how big the world really is. I still remember it. It took me hours, and he paid a pretty price! Well, the very next day, he came looking for me with a most unusual offer. Would I come back to their island? He told me about his small shop and that he wanted a seamstress who could adjust to a quiet life and, above all, mend sails.

"Of course I said yes. And that was how it happened. But do you want to know a secret?" she asked, smiling and lowering her voice. "To be honest, I never liked to embroider. I found it rather tedious, and I'd always hated my mother for making me learn. In the end, it was needles and threads that fed me. So, what did it matter that I liked to sew or not, or that Sergio was taken so stupidly? Not one bit. I was meant to live my life this way, and I did."

Old Woman Pérez fell silent at last.

"But how could you leave your daughter? Didn't you miss her?" Milagros blurted out finally. "While you were here working?"

Old Woman Pérez pursed her lips and considered the question. "Miss her?" she said, shrugging. "I did not think of this thing. I could have had my girl selling blouses on the street with me, like a beggar. Or given her to people who make maids of poor girls. Or worse," she said slowly, drifting off into thought. "I had a way to keep my girl safe and fed. And to do so, she had to be away from me. She is a happy woman now. That is all I can say about that."

She paused for a moment, sighed, and patted down her skirt. "I will tell you an important secret. Life does not unfold the way we expect, but that alone does not make it less wonderful. I thought my life would be one way. But it was not that way. Mine is not the only life story with a sad patch. And neither is yours, little one. No use pretending that you are the only person with a bad time. You are not. Perhaps Holly Pointe will give you a happy part of the story now . . . or perhaps another place. That will be up to you to decide."

Old Woman Pérez pushed herself slowly to a standing position, arched her back, and grimaced. "It's almost opening time, and I must get downstairs."

Milagros did not want the morning to end.

"But what about the pants? Don't you need to measure me and see what needs fixing?"

"No need. My eyes can see how you are built, Milagros."

Before Milagros could object, Old Woman Pérez hobbled to a large box and drew out a rectangle of folded orange tissue paper. "Here. Consider this a welcome present. It will be your size, I think. Meanwhile, I will fix these pants for you," she said, motioning to the table. "It is right that you should wear clothes that look like what the girls wear here in Holly Pointe. You can be a *norteamericana*. But it is not so bad to be from somewhere else or to look different from others around you. To have some color inside, this is a *good* thing. Maybe this present will look nice with the pants? A bit of old and a bit of new. Come on Monday. I'll have these for you then."

Old Woman Pérez winked and headed out the door, leaving Milagros alone.

Milagros ripped open the tissue paper and drew out a wide-sleeved gauzy blouse decorated with intricate fluorescent threads along the collar. Flowers perhaps? Balloons? Milagros held the blouse up to the window where the bright sun was shining over the bay. A tingle spread through her chest as she made sense of the strange pattern. No, these were not flowers at all.

All along the collar, Old Woman Pérez had embroidered a string of stingrays.

CHAPTER 24

Amigas

Milagros could scarcely wait to visit Old Woman Pérez again. Friendship had opened its fragrant bloom, and everything in her world seemed better. The shades of green on the new leaves were brighter, every breeze was more temperate. Even the crash of the sea outside her window became a simple mariner's tune that she whistled on the way to school.

When Monday afternoon arrived, she rapped cautiously on Day's front window and held out a present of three ripe tomatoes from her garden, beautiful ones with no vulgar bulges or splits in the skin. Her joy was contagious. Everything she had planted had come to fruit. Old Woman Pérez looked up from the sewing machine and, smiling, signaled her to go upstairs.

The door was unlocked, as if she had been expected. Waiting for her on the table were the pants, lengthened and neatly folded. Old Woman Pérez had permitted herself an embellishment: a charming embroidered hummingbird at the hip pocket, which Milagros noticed at once.

Even better was this: Next to the pants were two fried pastries, filled with cheese and tomatoes that warmed her inside. Milagros lingered at the apartment's railing from where she watched the lobster boats returning with their haul. She found it so peaceful among Old Woman Pérez's things, an oasis for reading the many books she liked to borrow from the school's shelves.

She pulled out from her sack a thin book she had found about shipwrecks and survivors.

After that, Milagros came every day after school.

*   *   *

"*¡Dios de mi alma!*" Old Woman Pérez cried as she stumbled on a pier board. She might have toppled completely if she had not leaned into her cane and grabbed Milagros's arm with all her might.

They had been walking along the pier telling stories, as they did every day. Old Woman Pérez was a masterful storyteller; every chapter of her life brimmed with drama. There was the hurricane of 1948, during which she and Sergio had held up the quivering walls of their house with only their bed slats. The quarantine against typhoid that turned neighbor against neighbor in her village. Her courtship with a young man conducted entirely through letters. The love affair had ended when, mistaken for another man, he was killed in a barroom dispute.

"A single shot pierced his heart, Milagros, right through my love letter that was in his breast pocket."

And then she had stumbled on the pier.

"Dr. Hughes tells me to exercise this hip, but it is of no help," she complained bitterly. "I tell him this always. Old wounds, they are forever. We simply learn to live with them."

Milagros steadied her carefully. "What happened? Was it an accident?"

"An accident? Not at all. I wrestled a burglar."

"No!" Another story was forming behind her friend's eyes, and Milagros was delighted.

"I was young and strong once, too," Old Woman Pérez said coyly. She shook her head in dismay. "I could never understand how Sergio was such a sound sleeper. He never heard the intruder in our house. But I did. I found him standing in our living room with his dirty fist wrapped around all our money. I wrestled my bills right out of his cowardly hand and chased him down the road with my kitchen knife. I let him get away—what lady wants to be a killer?—but not before he got in one good kick, the brute. This leg has hurt ever since. Nothing will change it."

Milagros guided her to a bench and helped her get seated. The knee was swelled, and the skin looked tight and shiny.

"Ginger and willow bark would help," Milagros told her, though she could not have explained how she knew this with the same absolute certainty that she knew the earth was a sphere. Rosa had used other remedies for bones that creaked. Nevertheless, Milagros felt sure. "Maybe John can find us some."

Old Woman Pérez only smiled and looked out over the water.

"Perhaps. . . . It is so sad to grow old and decrepit, Milagros. It's hard to find yourself white-haired and alone in the world."

Before she could reply, Milagros heard voices and looked up. Sara and Fang were coming down the boardwalk. They held buckets in their hands and fishing rods over their shoulders. Fang carried a small box of writhing bait worms.

"Miracle?" said Sara, leaving the boy behind and

ignoring Old Woman Pérez completely. "What are you doing with the sewing lady?"

"We are just walking for *señora*'s leg." Old Woman Pérez nodded and gave a short wave from the bench. "What are *you* doing with Fang?"

"My brother took us fishing in his skiff. I came to look for you, but you're never home. You should come with us tomorrow. You do know how to fish?"

Milagros nodded. When had she played last? Such an opportunity was appealing, but there was no use explaining about her afternoons with Old Woman Pérez. Holly Pointe was a place where old and young were kept separate. Milagros could read Sara's mind. *She's old. She's boring. She doesn't know about interesting things.*

"Maybe," Milagros whispered so that Old Woman Pérez would not hear.

Sara glanced at the bench and shrugged. "See you tomorrow, then."

Old Woman Pérez struggled to her feet and linked her arm through Milagros's bent elbow. She pointed her cane after Sara and Fang.

"This girl, Sara, she does not have good parents? Doesn't she know how to say *buenas tardes* to her elders?"

Milagros did not reply. She looked up at the darkening sky, worried that she would be late for dinner—again.

"We should go back, *señora*. It's late."

They walked in happy silence for a time, but when they were halfway to the shop, Old Woman Pérez stopped at a large white house on Greenwich Way. It was the home for the island's oldest residents, who were no longer able to live alone. John mowed its lawn weekly. Patty painted portraits to honor birthdays. On holidays, young students came to sing songs.

"A disgrace, but at least these *ancianos* haven't been sent to the mainland with strangers," she said. She was pointing to white-haired men and women scattered like litter on the pristine lawn. Some stared vacantly at the water; others fed stale bread to gulls. One woman in a pink sweater waved enthusiastically at Milagros and blew kisses.

"Poison me before I get there, yes?" Old Woman Pérez said. "I keep rat pellets beneath the sink."

"I will not!"

Old Woman Pérez gave a sad laugh. "For all the years I've been here, I cannot understand it. One gets old and useless. No one is available to take you in. Suddenly, you belong nowhere."

Milagros thought about this for a moment. Who would take care of Old Woman Pérez when she grew feeble? She wondered if Mercedes—somewhere far away—ever considered the question. Milagros took the time to study her friend. A strong nose and chin, the bright eyes. It was hard to imagine Elvirita Pérez ever becoming feeble.

"You're not useless. Or alone."

Old Woman Pérez looked up and patted Milagros's cheeks. "Yes? Well, that is very nice to hear. Neither are you."

She dropped Milagros's arm and turned toward the people watching them from their chairs. "I have some friends to visit now, Milagros. If you hurry, you might be able to catch Sara."

With that, she made her way slowly toward the residents who brightened as she approached.

"Good afternoon, good afternoon. It is a lovely day, yes?" Old Woman Pérez called happily as she reached for their hands in greeting. She looked like a baby among them.

Milagros smiled as she broke into a jog after Sara. No one was ever alone with Old Woman Pérez.

CHAPTER 25

Lobster Races

"Why are we here?" Diana complained.

The whole family was waiting inside Mr. Day's musty shop. Old Woman Pérez, finishing a project in the back room, had promised to be ready in a moment. Diana sniffled and rubbed at her swollen eyes. The bolts of fabrics were thick with dust.

"The lobster boat races start in ten minutes! If we're late, we'll miss the whole thing."

"Patience," John told her, though he glanced nervously down the street as the crowd continued to grow. The races were an annual family event in June and one that encouraged the only known gambling on Holly Pointe. He had bet his pride and money on *Leah's Wish*, the oldest among the boats, whose engine he had oiled and repaired himself.

"Do you think she'll be much longer?" Patty mused.

Diana was near madness. She tossed Milagros an ugly look. It had been Milagros who had insisted on inviting Old Woman Pérez for the event.

"What do you two do in this awful place every day?" Diana asked, flipping the sewing machine's levers in boredom.

Patty frowned at her daughter and lowered her voice to a whisper.

"Elvirita Pérez is a wonderful woman, Diana. I'm happy they're friends."

"What's so wonderful about her? She looks like a bent bicycle rim."

"That'll do," John said firmly. He tapped on the glass of the plate glass window and waved at his barber hurrying by.

"Don't insult my friend," Milagros warned.

"She can't be your friend. She's not your age. Right-headed people have friends their own age."

Milagros crossed her arms. She was in no mood for Diana's ill humor, and had never been one to allow abuse to go unchecked. She searched her heart for the perfect punishment, and before good sense stopped her, she unleashed it.

"Then why don't *you* have any friends?" she asked. "Not at school, not at home, not anywhere."

"I *do* so," Diana snapped.

"Girls—" John began.

"That's a lie," Milagros continued coolly. "No one at school likes you. Sara says you're a snitch. You just want everyone to be as miserable as you are."

Diana fell silent. Her lip quivered and her cheeks blazed red. The injured look on John's and Patty's faces made Milagros look away and pick at threads that were sticking to her shirt.

"Let's hurry on ahead, Diana," Patty said gently. "We'll be late." She kissed John on the cheek on her way to the door. "Meet us at the slips," she whispered.

Milagros listened for the jingling bells as the door closed behind them. She could feel John's eyes on her back.

"That was a rough thing to say," he told her.

Milagros did not immediately reply. This was his daughter—naturally he loved her best. There was no use pretending otherwise. She looked up at him uncomfortably. His hands were shoved deep inside his pockets.

"Diana is wrong to say those things to me about my friend."

"You are *both* wrong to hurt each other."

The sound of Old Woman Pérez's leg dragging on the dirty floor made her hurry a reply.

"Patty once said I am a girl with nothing. Well, now I have something that is my own. Diana has you and Patty. I have Señora Pérez." She looked into his eyes, dark as the ocean outside. "She is the only one here who can really be mine, isn't she?"

The curtain that led to the back room parted and Old Woman Pérez stepped through wearing a bright red cap and another of her lovely blouses.

"A wonderful day for the races," she said brightly. "Come along, Mr. Winters. We'll miss the excitement! Milagros and I have placed money on the *Sea Mist*."

☀ ☀ ☀

They jostled their way through the cheering crowds and the vendors who sold whittled pine egrets, birdhouses, and blueberry preserves. Milagros held Old Woman Pérez tightly by the elbow, as much to steady her friend as to relieve her own sudden nervousness among the horde that pressed all around her. The argument with Diana and John had left her gloomy, and now the shrill giddiness of the crowd was making things worse. Twice she had to shake from her mind the memory of the stilt walkers whose cowry shells she could still hear jangling in her mind. To calm herself, she took in deep breaths and fastened her gaze to the eight boats idling at the starting line.

Each captain had soaped down his boat, and even *Leah's Wish* looked lovely, banners fluttering from the wheelhouse, her rudder man freshly combed for the occasion. The captain waved happily to the Winterses from the stern. Families from all across the island had come with picnic baskets and homemade signs to urge on their favorite contender. Even the old residents had been parked like vehicles in a long row near the shore. The boats would go out to the distant channel markers and back.

With a single, ear-piercing shot in the air, Ned Granger started the races. The crowd roared their encouragements. Diana scrambled high on John's shoulders and shouted joyfully about the progress of *Leah's Wish*, which had taken an early lead. Patty sat away from them on one of the nearby pilings and sketched the subtle happy faces of the people she had known all her life. Old Woman Pérez whistled between her teeth like a sailor, even as the *Sea Mist* chugged and smoked dismally at the rear of the pack.

Milagros wandered away from them all. She noticed the shelter of a nearby poplar tree, and in a moment, she shimmied up the slick gray trunk and found a crook in which to hide and watch the boats. Even here at the happiest of island events she felt hollow. All she could think about was carnival day. Would memories of her old life always make her feel so apart from everything else?

As the boats rounded the buoys, she heard a whistle from below. Old Woman Pérez was waiting on the ground.

"You've found the best view of the races, I see. It's a pity I can't join you," she called.

After a few moments of silence, a voice called back from the safety of the leaves' thick camouflage.

"Do you think it's odd that we are friends, *señora*?"

Old Woman Pérez let out a big laugh. "Extremely!"

"Why? What's wrong with it?"

"Wrong? Who said wrong? It is only different. Though that is usually where trouble begins, yes? When something is different from what most people want to see."

The crowd shouted in fever pitch near the water and then erupted into applause. The smell of diesel fuel filled the air. A winner had reached the pier. Milagros squinted to see the name hand-painted on the stern. In a moment she scrambled down the tree and landed gently in front of her friend.

"The *Sea Mist* won!" Milagros said.

Old Woman Pérez took a deep, satisfied breath. "Of course she did. I know how to spot a winner." She picked leaves from Milagros's hair. "Now, let's picnic. I'm nearly dead with hunger."

"I don't want to eat with them," Milagros said quietly. John, flush-faced, was galloping toward them with Diana clinging to his back. Even at a distance, she could see Diana's eyes flashing hatred. The child was like a feral cat clawing and hissing for her rightful place and share.

Old Woman Pérez seemed not to hear. She spotted the men from the bait shop who were handling the winners' pay near the burning embers of cooking pits. "Come along, my dear friend," she said. "Roasted clams for the whole family. My treat."

CHAPTER 26

La Manta

"We ought to work on something together," Old Woman Pérez announced suddenly one day. She was rummaging through her sewing box for a smaller needle to finish the hibiscus she was embroidering on the collar of Milagros's white blouse. The blouse would be needed for the end of school assembly. In less than a week, summer would at last arrive.

Milagros looked up from her book. "Why?"

"Why not? Friends do things together, yes? Besides, it would help me with all these scraps. I can't bear to throw any of them out in case they still have some use. But these boxes are inching me out of this place. I think my old age is making me keep things like a squirrel." She pointed to the boxes scattered in the corner, each bursting at the edges.

Milagros had to agree; it was a mess, made worse by the breeze that was constant this close to the water. But she still shook her head.

"I don't know how to sew. Besides, we have such little time after school. And I really prefer John's garden," she said, thinking to herself that she had never seen Rosa sew so much as a button.

"Prefer? You can prefer something, but it should not be all that you can do, yes? Here, slide over that big box, and let's see what we have."

There was no point in arguing. Milagros sighed and did as she was told. She found the box, removing a small pile of mail that was stacked on top, including two letters, Milagros noted, postmarked from Mexico.

The two spread out the scraps on the floor, considering their options. It was an unseemly mix of denims, linens, velvets, cottons, jerseys, and twills—not enough of any single fabric to make a garment.

"I've seen bedcovers made from things like this here. Quilts," offered Milagros, thinking of the bedspread Patty had made her. The thought of such a chore hardly excited her.

"Bah—quilts are not just North American. They are made the world over. We've been making our quilts in Mexico for centuries. But let us think more. What we need is something a little more exciting than just a bed-cover, yes?"

They pondered the project for several days, drawing up ideas on folded napkins. Milagros grew more interested as they refined their thinking. They finally decided on a variation. Their creation would be a quilt in that it would be made from scraps. What choice did they have, with no piece bigger than a one-foot square? Still, they both were adamant: no pictures of flowers or flags or hearts. This quilt would be made to be worn like a shawl in the garden on cold days. It would have one corner hemmed over to become a hood if necessary.

"Like a very heavy *manta*," Old Woman Pérez said of the shawl. "And just to keep it exciting, let's create the pattern as we go. I hate knowing the end of things, don't you?"

For Milagros the quilt began as agony.

The first day she left for home with several deep pin-pricks that later got infected from garden soil and required peroxide.

"I can't do this," she complained often, sucking the blood from her fingertips.

Old Woman Pérez turned a deaf ear to her complaints.

"Use a thimble, *niña*. Like this."

"Angle the needle, more, more—that's right."

"That piece is no good for here. Try this blue one."

"That thread is too long; it will get knotted."

"Don't be lazy; put more stitches there."

On and on Old Woman Pérez instructed until at last Milagros could talk and stitch at the same time, her fingers dancing away from the sharp needle.

"Why don't you ever talk about your grandson? Or your daughter?" Milagros asked abruptly on the third day. She had noticed a new letter, unopened, again postmarked from Mexico. The pile of envelopes was growing larger, and her curiosity was piqued.

Old Woman Pérez stopped what she was doing and took the pins out of her mouth. "Héctor and Mercedes? They are well. What else would you want to know?"

"Are those letters over there from them?" She motioned to the pile.

Old Woman Pérez watched Milagros fastening a square of chenille. "Yes, the letters are from my family in Mexico. Tie that square on more tightly," she instructed Milagros.

She said nothing more about the letters or her daughter.

Mercedes certainly had a lot to say, Milagros thought, eyeing the stack. She was considering how to approach the topic again tactfully when Old Woman Pérez cleared her throat.

"Did I ever tell you the story about my teacher, the one who had only three fingers on her right hand?"

Milagros shook her head.

"Well, it begins with a girl—very bright—who was far too curious for her own good. . . ."

Old Woman Pérez spun her tale until all of Milagros's questions had been chased away. The stories took Milagros far from Holly Pointe. The hours passed, and square after square of fabric was pulled, trimmed, stitched, and tied until slowly the scraps from parkas, wedding gowns, and curtains began to take on a sensible pattern. It took form the way Patty's paintings took shape: mysteriously and with no warning.

When the piece was nearly done, they rested over a coffee.

"How do we finish it?" Milagros asked, running her fingers over the frayed edges. Her calloused fingers caught on the fabric.

"It should be something different, but strong enough to hold it together," Old Woman Pérez mused, taking a deep sip from her cup. "We'll have to consider this carefully."

Milagros was combing through two large boxes, but nothing seemed right. It was getting dark. The mosquitoes and black flies would make the walk home miserable if she waited much longer.

"Well, why don't we each think about it and bring an idea on how to finish it next time?" she said.

"Excellent. Let's see if our dreams find us a solution. Come back with your material tomorrow, and I will come with mine. The best idea wins. You know how I love a contest!"

"How will we know what's best?" Milagros asked.

"It will tell us," Old Woman Pérez answered confidently.

※ ※ ※

Milagros scoured her mind for the perfect idea. She ran her fingers along her curtain windows, stared at the edges of Sara's skirt, and even considered a torn net that John kept folded among his countless artifacts.

Late that night, however, she had an idea. She was dozing in the happy remembrance of Mrs. Mulligan's dismay when she breezed easily through lessons that taxed even Sara.

Then, the answer became clear.

Milagros tossed back her covers and crept toward the living room where a dim light was still burning. Patty was curled on the sofa with two cats. Colored pencils were spread on the coffee table; she was still sketching.

Ducking back into the bedroom, Milagros reached

under her bed. There, in the darkest corner, she found exactly what she was looking for and made her way nervously toward Patty.

"Trouble sleeping?" Patty asked when she saw her in the doorway. She put down her pad and rubbed her eyes. "I've lost track of time again. I hope the light didn't wake you."

"No."

Milagros took a step inside the room and gave the orange tabby a scratch under its chin. "What are you drawing?" she asked.

Patty hesitated a moment and held out her sketchbook. She had captured Diana's radiant smile as she sat on John's shoulders at the lobster boat races. The yellow of the girl's hair blazed against the sky. Love shone from John's dark eyes.

An unexpected wave of envy washed over Milagros. She had never assumed they would be her family, but now she was sure it would never be possible. She did not dare speak what they both knew was true. Only one person could give Milagros the undivided love she needed. She looked down at what she was holding and held it out to Patty. It was 12:30 A.M.—so late. She was nearly out of time.

"What are you doing with these?"

"I need your help," Milagros began awkwardly.

"How?"

"The *señora* and I are making a *manta* with old fabrics," she said, wanting urgently for Patty to understand. She pointed at the drawing of Diana and John. "It is the same way you paint the things and people you love. Our *manta* will be like our painting about friendship—"

But she did not need to finish. For the first time since they had met, Patty pulled her close.

※ ※ ※

The following day, Old Woman Pérez spread the unfinished quilt on the floor. It was a dazzling collection of triangles and squares that up close seemed a mess. But held at even a short distance, it looked like a stucco building in a market, layer upon layer of old posters and notices peeling off plaster.

"Why don't you go first, *señora*?" Milagros said.

Old Woman Pérez bent her head politely. "I am happy to offer this to finish our piece," she said very formally. She revealed a piece of lace, yellowed in spots with a rip near the bottom.

Milagros ran her fingertips over the intricate lace pattern.

"What is it?"

"This is the veil I wore on the day Mercedes was

baptized," she explained. "She was a fat and beautiful child." Old Woman Pérez studied the handmade lace for several minutes silently, lost in her own thoughts.

Milagros unzipped her sack. She pulled out a crisp white cotton blouse and a tan skirt. It was her school uniform—the blouse she had worn on the last day she lived on Las Brisas, the skin she had shed when she arrived. They were clean, neatly folded and pressed, exactly the way Señorita Alma would have required. Patty had washed and ironed them in the middle of the night, as Milagros had directed.

"My last clothes from home," she said simply.

The two stood awkwardly for a moment, and Milagros noticed that Old Woman Pérez's hands were trembling.

"They'll be more useful this way, *señora*. Much better than packing them away."

Old Woman Pérez cleared her throat.

"You are very right. There is no need at all for sentimentality about the past. It is done. We use this for our new quilt," she said. She grabbed up her scissors and opened them wide.

"To the future!" she said.

She made the first cut as Milagros carefully threaded their needles.

CHAPTER 27

The Red Bottle

"Well?"

Diana and Milagros sat blindfolded at the table. Standing before them in his overalls, an apron, and flowered oven mitts, John waited eagerly for their verdict. Pots, pans, and eggshells filled the sink. Steam was still rising from the pie pan on the table, filling the kitchen with the sweet smell of tomatoes, cheese, onions, and pastry crust.

John had been experimenting in the kitchen for the prize-winning recipe. Salsa, baked tomato casseroles, tomato muffins—even tomato ice cream. Milagros was starting to get sores on the inside of her mouth. This was his latest attempt. She chewed quietly and thoughtfully.

"It's good, Daddy," said Diana, pulling off her blindfold. "What is it?"

"What, indeed . . . ?" he said mysteriously. "What do you think, Miracle?"

Milagros let the wonderful morsel melt in her mouth, carefully avoiding the raw spot on the inside of her cheek. She had to admit, this was delicious. It would be lovely, she thought, especially on a cold day. Even now, almost at the start of summer, it was delectable. She felt a satisfied pride in her throat as she tasted the tangy tomato.

"Very good *pastel*, John."

"Thanks to you!" he said.

Milagros untied her blindfold and looked proudly at the succulent chunks of tomatoes against the light yellow of the eggs and crust.

"What is it?" asked Diana again, now picking through the pie with her fork.

John broke into a wide smile. "Really, it's tomato pie." He puffed out his chest dramatically as though speaking to a large crowd. "But I shall call this creation . . . *pastel de tomate* in honor of the youngest farmer to grow the best and earliest tomatoes this island ever saw! The Winters family wins first place, ladies and gentlemen!"

Milagros felt her cheeks blush. But one look at Diana told her she would pay for John's enthusiasm. Diana mumbled, "Bravo for the stupid tomato pie." She rose from her chair and headed out the door. "We'll have to hear about it all summer."

"Diana!" John called after her. "Wait!" The screen door slammed. "Patty might have handled that a little better, I suppose," he said sheepishly.

Milagros lowered her eyes and finished her pie. Patty had gone by ferry to the mainland that morning in search of art supplies. Left to navigate on his own, John would be at a disadvantage in this storm. She would have to watch for Diana's pranks carefully, she told herself.

"May I take a piece for later?" Milagros asked.

"Sure," he replied. He took a bite of his pie and let the morsel dissolve on his tongue. "More salt. A little less oregano?" he mused to himself.

Milagros did not mention that the *pastel de tomate* was for Old Woman Pérez, nor did she mention that she had been picking the very nicest vegetables off the vine before John ever had a chance to see them. She'd given them as presents and liked to think that he would approve.

"This is a winner," John said, interrupting her thoughts. "I don't know how you did it. Nobody but greenhouse growers have got a harvest yet! The tomato I used for this was the size of my whole fist! And it had almost no seeds. This will win for sure. But I think it still needs something. I'm going to try it again with more basil. Want to bring me a couple more from the garden? Then you can go do your errand. Oh, and you'll be down at the pier! You can watch them set up for the festival. I saw the ferry arrive yesterday." He turned to the refrigerator.

Milagros held her tongue. She knew Holly Pointe was preparing for the festival, but she was sure she would not go. Since her own terrible experience with the Rubians, she couldn't imagine ever going to a festival again. Leaving the shop the day before, she had watched the passersby gather on the lighthouse lawn to see the ferry unload. While the rest of the townspeople chatted happily about a summer spent eating fried doughnuts and fish fritters, Milagros had carefully watched the workers with their faces hidden under low-slung hats as they hauled in trunks and boxes, nets filled with stuffed toys. What was in the hearts of these workers? Her mind returned to Delfín. She would never be so blind again.

"Hey, dreamer?" John said, noticing her trance. "The tomatoes?"

"A la orden," she said politely. "Right away."

Milagros opened the door and headed to the garden.

She immediately noticed that John's scarecrow had been smashed, the broomsticks, hay, and hat strewn on the ground. *Diana.*

"Devil," Milagros muttered.

She worked her way toward the broken scarecrow along the fragrant rows of vegetables and marigolds, picking off determined worms as she saw them. The plants were thigh-high now, and the tomatoes and peppers hung like heavy Christmas ornaments off the vines. She reached out to pluck two large fruit and was surprised by a large toad sitting motionless in a puddle beneath a mound of marigolds. Its amber eyes were unblinking, even as she nudged it with her foot. It took one short hop closer to the middle of the plant, and turned its back, indignant.

Milagros crouched. She'd never been able to resist frogs or toads, even though they frightened Señorita Alma and most girls on Las Brisas ran shrieking at the sight. Maybe that was why she loved them: because so many people didn't. Couldn't they see these creatures were magicians? They began as one thing and ended as another thing entirely. They learned to breathe air, the very thing that would have killed them at one time. Ugly or not, you had to admire them.

For a moment, she wondered how Diana might feel

finding this little fellow in her pillow. The thought of Diana shrieking made Milagros smile.

She pulled the tomatoes free and turned toward the house. John was in the window, kneading more dough. He waved a sticky hand.

She never saw Diana on the other side of the fence, fumbling through the scarecrow's shirt pocket. Nor did Milagros hear the high-pitched whizzing of the object hurtling through the air in her direction.

It hit her squarely on the temple with a dull thud and sent a sensation of pins and needles across her forehead. She stumbled and reached down for the curious object at her feet—even as her vision grew fuzzy and the blood dripped into her eyes. A sickening thrill ran through her stomach. Was she dreaming?

It was a red bottle, and inside, a small message. Her knees buckled, and her vision grew dim. Drops of her blood seeped into the ground near her feet as she struggled to make her hands work. She fumbled with the bottle, but could not get the message out. Finally, she let out a deep breath and her body fell forward. Lying on the ground, she tried to focus her eyes on the message in the bottle. She thought she could make out the words: *Rosa vive.*

"*Dios mío*, help me," she cried softly.

She closed her eyes and fell unconscious.

The secret was released at last. Miguel's message made the air gust sharply, banging all the shutters and screen doors in a frightening clatter as Diana ran. The bottle near Milagros's head shattered into hundreds of ruby bits. With the second blast of wind, it gathered fury and swirled into a red cloud over Milagros before seeping within the crevices of the cliffs to wait.

CHAPTER 28

The Cursed Ship

It was a curse. That was the only explanation El Capitán could point to with certainty. And now Miguel de la Torre would have to pay.

El Capitán leaned on a large walking stick that had notches all along its length—one for each week of this dreaded scourge. He sawed his knife across the stick at the very bottom. El Capitán had reached the end of the stick. It was time for action.

Once again, the sky was cloudless and the water deathly still. As it had for weeks, the *Ruby Sails* bobbed aimlessly like a cork. Not a single vessel had passed this particular expanse, though these waters had always been a fruitful spot for his pirates. But for many weeks now, no opportunity had presented itself for a thrilling chase, for a robbery, for a chance to abscond with food and supplies. Even the rusted fishing boats, so common in these waters, had vanished. Now, the hungry men lay about sleeping like drunkards in a slum, dreaming of sweet water and fried ham. When the provisions were gone, they would begin to turn on each other. El Capitán knew this from experience. All alliances ended with thirst and hunger. And with evil men, they would only end violently.

El Capitán picked at his brown teeth with the tip of his knife and let Miguel squirm in expectation. The only sound on the ship was the lapping of the water and the incessant scraping of a chain.

"Do you see this, De la Torre?" he said at last, pointing his knife at the stick.

Miguel eyed the walking stick but said nothing. Since the night that he had encountered the manta ray, he had fallen into a despondent state. He spoke to no one and skulked around the ship like a fearful dog. He had stopped visiting Rosa altogether, leaving her care to the lookouts. He failed to eat even the hard biscuits that were still available. Now his ribs were piercing his skin, and his face was gaunt. It took all his energy just to stand before El Capitán.

"It is a calendar, De la Torre. A calendar of trouble."

Miguel stared blankly.

"Do you know what I think, De la Torre? I think that our troubles are right here on this ship. I think that our troubles are right here where we are standing. I think that our troubles come from a curse. And I think our curse is *you*."

Miguel could not help but give out a tiny snort. He? The source of a powerful curse? If only it were possible to have such power, he would actually be a much happier man.

"There is only one way for a pirate to deal with a curse, De la Torre. Do you know what it is? It is to make an offering to the sea. It is to do the unthinkable."

Miguel almost brightened. Perhaps he would die a true pirate's death after all, he thought. Walk out on the plank at sword point and jump into the jagged teeth of the sharks at dusk. At least he could die heartlessly if he had not managed to live that way.

"I am prepared to die, Capitán."

"Die? You?" El Capitán laughed. "Oh, no. That would not do at all. Have you forgotten that a pirate can read people's hearts? And this is what I find in yours: You are an abysmal failure as a pirate, De la Torre. You still feel pity. You cringe to know that someone is in pain. You might steal a gold coin but will surely put a silver one in its place. And so you are worthless to this ship. This I have known for a long time. So kill you? No. No, that is not the solution. The way to regain a pirate ship's menace is to exact cruelty in its highest form. We must do that which will break a kind heart forever."

Miguel considered what that might be until he heard

the scraping of Rosa's chain. A new, horrible thought came into focus. His stomach tightened. His eyes darted quickly to the ceiling. The sound stopped directly above the spot where he and El Capitán were standing.

El Capitán smiled and let his eyes travel to the same spot in the ceiling. "Ah, well, at least you are not stupid, then. Yes, De la Torre," he growled. "I have discovered some very interesting things about you. You have a bit of a soft side, eh? You have visited our little slave at night, washed her wounds, tended to her. No, don't deny it. It's no use. She has confessed."

He let his voice drop and spoke through clenched teeth. "What's more: I have had a long chat with the lookout, and I have done some digging. You can imagine my surprise when I learned from those stupid Rubians that this woman is none other than your wife!"

Betraying himself at last, Miguel let out a small gasp, heavy with his despair.

"So here is how it will be now, you weakling," El Capitán spat. "Your dear wife dies tomorrow at high noon. And it will be you who will feed her to the fishes."

El Capitán threw back his head and laughed. Overhead, the chains dragged once more.

CHAPTER 29

The Patient

Milagros awoke to a viselike grip around her head and a throbbing pain that allowed her to open only one eye halfway. She lay in her bed and looked around slowly. Two empty chairs sat next to her bed as though she were expecting visitors. How long had she been here? What had happened? She ran her fingers tenderly along the side of her head. Coarse thread stuck out like small quills near her eyebrow and extended almost to her ear.

John entered carrying a tray of cookies and a hot steaming mug.

"Oh, thank goodness. Here, try this. I just made it. Tomato tea. Lots of vitamin C," he said, setting the tray in front of her.

Milagros smiled weakly and tried to prop herself up on her elbows, but a sharp pain shot through her head. She lay back down.

"*Ay, ay, ay,*" she moaned.

"Hold on a minute, Miracle." John put an extra pillow behind her shoulders and gently lifted her back up until she was almost in a sitting position.

"You're going to have quite a shiner there," he said, pointing to her sore head. "Dr. Hughes came by and stitched you. You'll be fine in a couple of days, but you'll have to miss school and take it easy for a while."

"What time is it?" Milagros asked.

"Nearly six. You've been out for hours. Gave me a good scare, I can tell you that."

"What happened?" she asked.

"I was about to ask you the same," he said. "One minute you were standing outside, and the next minute you were in a bloody heap!"

Milagros closed her eyes painfully. The insides of her eyelids seemed to glow. "Diana," she said.

John's face tensed. "Diana?"

Milagros tried to piece together the events, but she could not say for sure what had happened.

"I saw her, I think. I don't know. There was a bottle," she began unsteadily. Or had she dreamed it?

"A bottle?" he repeated.

She was about to speak when there was a knock at the front door. John hurried to answer it, and when he returned, he was followed by Old Woman Pérez. She was carrying a thermos in one hand and a large sewing bag in the other.

She cupped Milagros's face in her hands, traced the sign of a cross on her forehead, and surveyed the damage like a general.

"Nothing a little aloe and cornmeal won't fix."

"Actually, Dr. Hughes left this, Mrs. Pérez," said John, holding out the tube of antibiotic ointment in her direction. "She won't need any more for a while. What I do need is for her to drink a little bit. Just to be sure she's all right." He shrugged sheepishly and lowered his voice. "And I need to find Diana."

Old Woman Pérez ignored the ointment. She sat on the edge of the bed, glanced disapprovingly at the odd tomato tea, and unscrewed the lid of her own thermos instead. She poured a small cup of hot milk that smelled lightly of cinnamon and handed it to Milagros. Then she pulled out a tiny cone of incense and lit it on the nightstand. A thread of pungent smoke coiled toward the ceiling.

She turned to John. "I will sit here for a little while with Milagros, Mr. Winters. I have some sewing with me, and Milagros and I like to share stories. We can pass the time pleasantly. It is a wonderful thing for an old woman like me to have someone to share stories with."

She patted Milagros's legs and smiled at John. "And besides, Milagros tells me you are preparing to win the festival." She took a deep breath. "The smells in this house today are heavenly."

John smiled shyly. He looked at Milagros a bit reluctantly. "Okay with you, Miracle?"

"Yes. I am fine with Señora Pérez."

"Oh, and Mr. Winters? You will find Miss Diana hiding in Milagros's dinghy."

"What?" Milagros cried in alarm. She tried to get up.

John held up a calming hand to Milagros. He peered out through the curtain at the dinghy overturned at the edge of the cliff. "I can't see her."

"Look closely, Mr. Winters, at the yellow patch in the boat. Miss Diana."

John recognized the blond hair at last. "What on earth is she doing there?" He looked sadly at Old Woman Pérez and then fell silent, thinking.

She smiled gently. "Go to her, Mr. Winters. Fear and sadness are terrible things. Nothing good ever comes of them."

When he had closed the door behind him, Old Woman Pérez turned to Milagros.

"Naturally, I came as soon as I heard you'd been hurt," she said quietly in Spanish, settling herself into a chair. She reached into the bag and pulled out a large white blanket. Around three sides, lovely balloons had been embroidered. She unfastened a thick needle and got to work on a red balloon. "Mrs. Hughes came by the shop with the doctor's Sunday pants. I always tell them the front pleats are not so flattering for a man with a large stomach. But again, they ask for hems on pleated pants." She shook her head in disapproval.

"In any case, Mrs. Hughes mentioned her husband had been by to see you for a small accident. But of course, I know, this is no accident. Miss Diana's tricky hand is in this somewhere. So? What happened here today?"

Milagros tried to recount the events as best she could, but nothing seemed to make sense. Her memory was broken into little pieces.

"I don't really know what happened to me," she said, exasperated. "But I'm sure Diana has something to do with it."

Old Woman Pérez pursed her lips and nodded. "Obviously."

"I'm through with her," Milagros spat. "I can be just as hateful! I'll be much better at it than she is."

"Better at hating and hurting someone?" Old Woman Pérez asked, a bit surprised. "This is not something to be good at. It is like metal wanting to rust the fastest. *¡Ay!*"

Old Woman Pérez put her pricked finger in her mouth. "I'm growing old and careless."

Milagros closed her eyes sullenly. Thoughts of getting even with Diana were still flooding her aching head. She tried again and again to put the events in order.

Old Woman Pérez set down her work and crossed to the window. A smile crept across her face.

"They've brought the Corriedale sheep from Berry Island. They make the loveliest blankets from their wool. If you look carefully you can see them grazing on the grass near the lighthouse." She turned back to Milagros. "This festival season will be very wonderful, you'll see. They have fastened posters all over town. I've brought one here," she said, tapping her dress pocket. "And do you know there is a quilting contest this year? We can enter our *manta* now that it is finished."

Milagros took a sip of hot milk and refused to reply.

Old Woman Pérez continued. "Don't look so glum. You will be better in a week's time. The festival will be here all summer. You'll still be able to go."

"I will not go to the festival." Milagros leaned her head back into the pillow and closed her eyes. "I don't like carnivals."

Old Woman Pérez frowned. "Ah, I see now. It is this question of what we like to do again. Well, that is a shame to miss the fun. Mr. Winters will be counting on you to watch him win the cooking prize. What will you do about that?"

Milagros shrugged. It would be hard to disappoint John Winters.

Old Woman Pérez stayed quiet a moment. "And then there is the matter of our quilt. Do you know, I have never won anything. It might be nice." She paused and thought for a moment. "I could go with you if you like," she offered quietly. "I think I can manage most things—except those silly sack races, perhaps. Although I think you will have other friends who may want you to go, yes?"

Milagros smiled at the thought of Old Woman Pérez in a race. But she also knew how silly it was in the north for a twelve-year-old girl to be in the company of an old woman at a festival. Besides, she wasn't going; her mind was made up. She had already told Sara as much.

"Maybe next year," she offered, stifling a yawn.

Old Woman Pérez waved her hand, losing patience at last. "Don't be silly. A year can change everything. The festival is now," she said with authority. "We'll go. And here—to give you something to look forward to—here is an advertisement. I took it off the pole outside the shop this morning. You can look at it when your head is not so sore, yes?" She pulled out a bright red flyer from her pocket.

Milagros squinted to get a better look: HOLLY POINTE SUMMER FESTIVAL. Milagros felt her eyelids begin to droop; the headache was exhausting. She tried to imagine happy faces, but her thoughts kept returning to a bottle. Soon, she could feel herself slipping into a dream.

"There was a bottle, and it said '*Rosa vive*,'" she said sleepily.

Old Woman Pérez furrowed her brow. "Hush, now. We can sort it out in the morning."

"A red one, I think. Do you know anything about red bottles, *señora*?" Milagros asked again as sleep overcame her. "Or stingrays?" She felt herself drift off.

"Rest now," Old Woman Pérez said as she watched Milagros take in deep, long breaths. "That warm milk will be doing the trick soon." She folded the flyer in half and placed it like a small tent on the nightstand.

Old Woman Pérez tucked the blankets around Milagros snugly. She wondered how many times her own daughter, Mercedes, had gone to bed without her mother smoothing the sheets and chasing away nighttime monsters. She felt sadness push against her throat.

Old Woman Pérez looked out at the festival grounds in the distance. The truth was this: She loved the festival. It was one of many things she had learned to enjoy about Holly Pointe. The quiet people, the simplicity of her days, even the rhythm of the fierce seasons. And now, of course, there was Milagros.

Still, she could not deny that she had also enjoyed her trip back to her daughter. It felt like home even after so many years away. When did a new place finally begin to feel like home? Maybe never, she mused.

She stood at the window, daydreaming about the sounds of Mexico, the voices of friends, the colors in the sky, the familiar food, the afternoons under a palm tree. Her daughter was a beautiful woman now, more beautiful still when she held her precious baby. Luckily, those two would not be parted. They wouldn't have to think about each other across miles and oceans, wondering what the other might be thinking and doing. They would have no regrets.

As Old Woman Pérez's mind drifted, she patted her pocket absently. Inside was the letter she had received from her Mercedes that morning—the third such letter in a month.

Always, always it was the same insistent request.

Mamá, it is time for us at last to make up for all the years we were not together. I could use your help. Come back. Be with your daughter and grandson. We need you. Come home to us, Mamá.

CHAPTER 30

Danger in the Mist

Milagros awoke the next day with a start. It was the last day of school, and the house was eerily quiet. Outside her window, the sky was clear, the water calm. But she felt the hair at the back of her neck bristle and a tightening in her stomach as though she were about to plummet from a cliff. Something was terribly wrong.

There was no tray on her nightstand. No chairs near her bed. Not even the flyer. John had cleaned up while she slept.

Milagros closed her eyes to put together all the shards of her memory that were now clear. Diana had thrown a bottle, one that bore Rosa's name.

And though Diana claimed to know nothing, she had rushed off to school before Milagros could properly interrogate her in the privacy of their room. Ignoring her pounding headache, Milagros took advantage of the solitude. She ransacked Diana's drawers, her closet, and under her bed. She upended sofa cushions and opened every cabinet door, despite cats who swiped at her for the disturbance. She was rummaging beneath the parlor sofa when she heard the kitchen door open. In a moment, Patty was in the room. She gasped in fright when she saw Milagros lying on her stomach.

"Are you all right? What are you doing out of bed?" she cried.

Milagros struggled to her feet, but the room was spinning.

Patty steadied Milagros by the elbow and led her back to the bedroom. After she had tucked the blankets around Milagros tightly, she crossed her arms and sighed.

"I'll have to keep watch here all day," she said a bit crossly. She leaned over to examine Milagros's swollen forehead and grimaced. The tender bruise extended all the way around the right eye and cheek. She softened her voice. "Does it hurt very much today?"

Milagros shook her head, though, in truth, her head was splitting.

Patty surveyed the opened drawers.

"Looking for something?"

Anger welled up inside Milagros. "Yes. Diana has something that belongs to me. Something important."

"Ah," Patty said, sighing. "A red bottle, by any chance?"

Milagros snapped to attention.

"John told me all about what happened here yesterday," Patty continued. "I'm ashamed of both of you girls."

Milagros spoke through her teeth. "Ashamed of *me*, Patty? Why? I did nothing wrong. I did not throw a bottle at anyone." She pointed at her forehead. "I did not do this."

Patty blushed. "And Diana says she didn't do it either. I know you and Diana aren't friends; I know that she's been difficult. But the fact is, there is no red bottle in the yard, Miracle. Not even the tiniest piece of one. Diana says she has never seen such a thing. How can John and I accuse her of something so awful when we have nothing to prove it?"

Milagros did not respond.

Patty lowered her voice to a whisper.

"I don't think you're a liar, Miracle, if that's what you're thinking. Maybe Diana did mean to hurt you in a moment of anger. But red bottles hidden away and used as a weapon? Impossible."

Milagros turned away.

"I am so tired now, Patty," she said abruptly. There

was no point in arguing with parents who adored their children. "I am going to sleep again."

Patty was quiet for a long while, but Milagros would not open her eyes. Finally, she rose and called from the door.

"Stay in bed, Miracle. Promise me. You're not steady enough yet."

"I promise you," she muttered.

"I'll be in the shed working."

Milagros lay perfectly still. When she heard the screen door close, she crept to the window and watched Patty walk through the pine woods to her shed.

Then Milagros considered her scarce options.

Diana most certainly knew something about the bottle that bore her mother's name. If it wasn't in the house or garden, then it must be hidden at school. Milagros would have to find a way to rummage through Diana's things there, and she had no time to lose. If necessary, she would confront Diana alone and wrestle from her whatever truth she could.

She dressed quickly and stepped out the front door into the bright June day. Immediately, she crouched out of sight and crept on all fours through the overgrown grass.

When she reached the road, she stood slowly. Again

the world seemed to spin, and she noticed that her wound was moist with new blood. Should she turn back? *No,* she told herself. She would find the red bottle first— prove to John and Diana that she was no liar, find Rosa's whereabouts.

She had not gone far when she found that she had to lean against a tree once again. Something was wrong, and it was not simply her throbbing headache or the world moving in double. An acrid scent was in the air, and worry was again at her neck.

Honking geese crossed the cloudless sky on their way back for the summer weather. Turning up the collar of her jacket, she moved on, leaning into a gust that appeared from nowhere and pushed against her as if trying to hold her back. Milagros pressed on.

The wind grew more insistent as Milagros made her way down island. Each time she stopped to rest, she studied the clouds that had appeared on the horizon suddenly. Gulls that normally sat fluffing their feathers on fences and pilings, now flapped nervously out to sea. *Island weather changes in a moment,* she had often heard John say. A chilly rainstorm now would make the walk much worse, she thought as she hurried on. She was more than halfway to the school.

She had walked for almost a mile when she realized

that the road and houses appeared muted and dream-
like. She wondered if it was her vision that was altering
their appearance and sat down again on a large boulder,
waiting for the feeling to pass. It was when she opened
her eyes and looked down at her shoes that she immediately understood what was really happening.

Her feet had disappeared inside a cottony mist that
hovered just above the grass.

Fog.

She hated this strange mist, feared it, knew all about
its pirates—and now she was far from home and at its
mercy. She forced herself to her feet and rushed on as
best she could. But with each step she took, the mist
inched higher to swallow her. Her knees disappeared,
then her waist and chest. Soon she held a hand to her face
and saw nothing. The road ahead vanished completely.

Milagros swallowed her fear and stumbled along
with her arms outstretched before her. Foghorns
sounded over the water as she tried to make her way by
memory. Urgent whispers and laughter were gathering
in the mist, but Milagros refused to listen.

I won't be afraid, she told them angrily. *You are only
pirates; cowards, one and all. I too have pirate blood in my veins,*
she threatened them privately. *I can be as strong and ruthless as you.*

All the same, she broke into a blind run toward the school.

How long had she been traveling? She could not tell. Even as she ran with all her might, time seemed to stop. The fog thickened into a labyrinth all around her, and she lost her bearings completely. Should she go left? Right? On clear days, the barn's red siding and white trim made the school visible from miles away. But now, Holly Pointe School, like everything else on the island, was indiscernible. Milagros forced herself to continue as a cold sweat ran down her spine. Every inch of her felt danger.

Just then, the school bell pierced the fog. Its riotous clanging sent the dire warning into the air. *Beware! Danger!*

She knew the school was not far off. She waited for each peal and ran blindly toward the sound. At last she saw a hint of pink behind the haze. Children were running and squealing in terror somewhere in the yard.

"Inside, everyone!" someone called. It was Mrs. Mulligan's sharp voice. "Inside until the fog passes. No stragglers!"

The air was impenetrable now and heavy with a scent of unfathomable sadness. Milagros groped until her hands found the side of the building. She edged along its rough exterior, struggling to find the door that would lead her safely inside.

Suddenly, Mrs. Mulligan stepped out from the mist like an apparition. She was uncombed and perspiring, and her face was pale. All around her, children were racing for the building, their faces contorted in fear. Diana, among them, came to a halt when she saw Milagros. She was wide-eyed and reached for Mrs. Mulligan's hand for comfort.

"What are you doing here, Miracle?" Mrs. Mulligan rasped. "Get inside. There is danger."

Milagros shook her head. She stared past her teacher into the yard at an even more frightening view.

The mist behind Mrs. Mulligan was turning from white to a bright crimson, the color of rubies, of anger and hatred, of spilled blood.

Diana's eyes followed Milagros's gaze.

"What's happening?" she cried and backed away from the mist that crept toward her in long tendrils. "Why does it look this way?"

But Milagros had no time to reply. Mrs. Mulligan had lurched forward to grip her arm.

"What curse have you brought to us?" the teacher gasped. Her eyes widened, and she moved a trembling hand to clutch her chest. She collapsed with a dull thud at the girls' feet.

Diana took several steps away, staring in disbelief at Mrs. Mulligan's still body. Then she glared at Milagros.

"Help!" she screamed. "Help! Miracle has hurt Mrs. Mulligan! Help!"

The commotion was now at impossible heights. Milagros could not separate the children's screams from Diana's voice . . . nor that from the laughter she was sure she heard coming from inside the dreadful red haze. Mrs. Pennington appeared, groping the ground to find Mrs. Mulligan.

"Mildred!" She put two fingers on Mrs. Mulligan's neck, and then put an ear to her chest. "Someone, anyone! Get help! There's no heartbeat!"

CHAPTER 31

On the Run

"Run!"

That was the only word Milagros yelled as she snatched Diana away from the red veil that was now rolling toward them.

"Stop! Come back!" a voice called out after them. But Milagros did not heed. She looked back only once to see Mrs. Pennington disappearing inside the red fog; the teacher would have no choice but to turn her attention to Mrs. Mulligan. Milagros shuddered as she thought of the wounds to Mollie's hind legs. What terrible hurt had come to the old woman?

She clamped her hand around Diana's wrist and sped down the road as the school bell sounded a mayday signal that echoed across the island. Soon Ned Granger's police jeep sped by. Milagros yanked Diana behind a tree to let it pass.

They ran until their sides were bursting, until Milagros's eyes were clouded with blood, until her wobbly legs could scarcely hold her steady. At last, the dim lighthouse beam came into view. There was no time to get home safely before the rolling fog reached them. They would have to hide.

"This way," Milagros cried, pointing beneath a small dock, away from the festival workers who were huddled inside their tents taking cover from the alarming mist. The girls sped under the pier and finally crouched behind three boulders that were covered in seaweed. Their feet were only inches from the water, and the smell of clams and dead fish was overwhelming. No one would see them there, Milagros hoped. Perhaps, not even pirates.

Diana was terrified and furious. She yanked free at last and regarded Milagros, who lay gasping.

"Why have you dragged me here?" she demanded, catching her breath. "What's happening?"

Milagros closed her eyes and searched for the patience that would keep her from driving a fist right into the younger girl's jaw. For an insane moment, she had thought Diana might thank her for saving her from danger, perhaps apologize for nearly killing her with a bottle, willingly tell her what she knew about the message that Milagros was sure she had seen. Instead, she was making demands.

"Have you done this to us?" Diana quaked. "Mrs. Mulligan is right! It's you! You brought this awful fog! Witch!"

"Shut up," Milagros ordered. She lunged at Diana with the very last energy she had and grabbed a fistful of her shirt. She put her bloody and swollen face close and growled.

"I have no idea what is in this mist or why it's here. But I can tell you that it's evil, and it has to do with my parents. Tell me about the bottle from my father's ship," Milagros hissed.

"What are you talking about?" Diana asked.

Milagros leaned in and snarled. "I know it was you who hit me with that bottle. I know that bottle has my mother's name, Rosa. I saw it. It said, 'Rosa lives.' You're going to tell me where my mother is now, or I will let you die out here in the mist just like Mrs. Mulligan! These ghosts will tear at you the way they did Mollie."

Diana looked ashen. Milagros shook her hard.

"Tell me about the bottle!" she shouted, pointing to her cut. The new wound had opened and blood was trickling down the side of her face. "It had my mother's name in it. It was a message for me. My God, Diana! I know you understand what it is to love a mother and father. I see how you love yours and how much they love you. Rosa is the only thing that I have. Tell me where my mother is or I—I will crash your head on these rocks!"

Diana was shaking. "I don't know anything, I swear. I found the bottle on the rocks—that's all. I was going to tell you!"

Milagros threw her back in disgust. "But you wanted me to suffer first."

They were interrupted by men's voices and the pounding of heavy shoes. Through the slats in the pier, they saw beams of light from flashlights. Up close, Milagros recognized the brown trousers of a police officer and a familiar pair of faded blue jeans and worn sneakers. John and Officer Ned Granger.

Milagros clamped a hand over Diana's mouth. The girls were motionless as the footsteps stopped above their heads. If she'd slid her fingers through the boards, Milagros could have touched John's foot.

"Check the tents," Ned Granger ordered. Footsteps sounded.

"I can't explain this," said John miserably. "Why have they run off?"

"Who can tell what an Away girl will do?" Ned

Granger's voice answered. "It's something she's done, John. Hurt Mrs. Mulligan, most likely."

"I don't believe that."

Officer Granger was undeterred. "No? What do you know about this girl? Almost nothing. Fact is, we've got a crisis, and it points to her. A teacher collapsed, and your own girl missing. You and Patty should have listened, John. Cases like these . . . Away people, they're not to be trusted."

"Stop talking nonsense, Ned. The girls are afraid. There's been bad weather and trouble between them. They're afraid and lost in this mess. Can we just concentrate on finding them, please?" said John tersely.

The footsteps receded as the two men walked off the pier. Diana ripped free Milagros's hand and edged toward the open air.

"Well, they're going to send you back to Away for sure," she said over her shoulder. "I'm going to tell Daddy that I had absolutely nothing to do with this. And I'm going to tell him that you threatened to kill me," she said. "He'll hate you."

Diana turned to glare at Milagros. But she was already gone.

CHAPTER 32

Rosa's End

When Miguel came to Rosa at noon, his skin was pale and his hands trembled. Rosa had been made ready. A thick rope coiled around her body, trapping her arms and legs. Only her feet and head were exposed.

"*¡Vamos, mujer!*" he whispered. Let's go, woman. His hands shook as he hoisted her over his shoulder like a sack of rice and then set her down and steadied her on the gangplank.

The other pirates stood across the deck; El Capitán stood tall near the ship's wheel. An expectant silence hung over the ship. All around them, the sky glowed crimson.

"Walk," Miguel ordered softly.

Rosa moved her feet in tiny steps as the plank beneath her bobbled. Miguel walked closely behind her.

Give our child hope, Rosa had said. What disastrous advice, he thought, fool's advice that had pierced his heart like arrows. And for what? Now Rosa would perish at his hand as punishment. And for him it was even worse. He had even failed at being a failure.

"Behold, pirates," shouted El Capitán. "We offer to the sea a most horrible act. Let the curse be lifted from this vessel." The pirates stared in awe.

Rosa turned carefully to face Miguel, who held a small sword in her direction. She looked at him not with fear, but with pity.

He looked nervously into the ocean for sharks that he knew would be circling below.

Then, without a word, he gave Rosa one hard shove with the point of his sword.

She fell almost gracefully, her eyes closed, smiling. And then, to the shock of El Capitán and the others, Miguel de la Torre jumped in after her.

Miguel reached for her as they sank into the still water. He wanted to save her, to tell her at last that he was sorry for his weakness, that he was ashamed of what he had done to their daughter, that he had tried to undo the unspeakable harm.

"Forgive me!" he cried.

But as Miguel reached toward his wife, he found

only loose rope. As the nose of the first hungry shark bumped him, he turned and saw a large shape hovering nearby. There, near the ship's stern, swam a most glorious pink ray, its enormous wings pulsing to safety.

"Devil ray!" he heard someone shout from the deck.

But Miguel knew the wonderful truth as the sharks circled and he prepared to die.

Rosa's love had been stronger than all his hate and sorrow. She was free.

CHAPTER 33

Desaparecida

The door to Old Woman Pérez's apartment was locked, but Milagros remembered where her dear friend kept a spare key. It was hidden under a rusty El Pico coffee can she kept on the stoop to catch rainwater for her window plants. It had been Milagros's idea to teach her how to keep a window garden. *Water keeps things from dying; rain makes things live,* Milagros had taught her the first day. The difference between surviving and thriving.

She knocked urgently at first and, getting no answer, put the key into the lock and let herself in. She shut the door quietly behind her. The curtains were drawn, and the apartment was much darker than the awful red daylight outside. Milagros let her eyes adjust.

"*¿Oye? Soy yo,*" she called. Hello? It's me.

No one replied. Where could her friend be? Was she safe? Maybe Old Woman Pérez was still working downstairs. She started to cross to the window but stopped dead in the center of the room. Something was different. What?

Milagros let her eyes roam across the room for clues. The apartment was neatly picked up for one thing. No threads lingered in the corners. The counters were completely cleared of the dishes, cups, and utensils that usually lay about. The boxes of scraps were closed, the seams sealed with transparent packing tape. Their quilt was folded neatly into a large square on the bed.

Milagros walked around slowly, rolling the possibilities in her mind. Where was Old Woman Pérez? Was she safe from this terrible fog?

She spied an open envelope on the bare table and reached for it. It was exactly like the others she had seen from Mexico. It was private correspondence; of course she knew this. But Milagros was far too curious. She sat on the bed near the quilt, pulled out the letter, and read what Mercedes had been asking of her mother for months.

Milagros read and reread a single line at the end: *Come back. We need you.*

She felt the last of her strength leave her. It was clear to her now. How had she allowed herself to be so fooled into trusting someone? Old Woman Pérez had returned to her family in Mexico. She had not even said good-bye. Milagros lay down on the bed and pulled the quilt up over her head.

CHAPTER 34

Strange Occurrences

What Milagros did not know at that dark moment was that her friend was on a most important errand. Old Woman Pérez had spent the morning looking for a suitable trunk, something large and sturdy in which to pack up her boxes of clutter. She was not packing to move—she was making room for Mercedes and Héctor.

I cannot possibly come, Mercedes, for life has proven itself so complicated here in this little town. There is a girl here, a girl who is alone, whom you and little Héctor should meet. And so the letter went on to explain why it was Mercedes who should come and live in Holly Pointe, instead. She hoped Mercedes would agree.

Old Woman Pérez was standing in the back room of Millie's Secondhand Store when the salesman noticed that she looked dreadfully ill. They had just been considering the merits of a large leather trunk—a black affair with wide straps and silver buckles—when the first hints of red mist had surprised them. She suddenly stopped talking and stared out the store's plate glass window.

"Look at that!" the salesman said in awe. "Can't say we ever get so unusual a color."

Old Woman Pérez did not answer.

He noticed that his customer was now covered in perspiration, her face pale. She had dropped her purse, and the contents were dashed on the carpet at her feet.

"Ma'am?" he asked. "Are you all right?"

He stared outside to see what the woman was looking at. There was nothing visible outside. Everything that had been there moments before had vanished: mothers with babies, the mailman making his rounds.

"Do you smell it?" Old Woman Pérez asked him, holding her chest, remembering the days when she missed Mercedes with unspeakable agony. The tightening was like a terrible sting, growing larger and more painful by the moment.

"No, ma'am. I don't smell anything. What do you mean?"

"Roses, of course. The smell is everywhere, yes?"

"It's the rugosas that are blooming, ma'am. It's that time of year." The salesman put his hand on Old Woman

Pérez's elbow and steered her toward a chair behind the register. "Wait here."

He rushed to the phone at the counter and dialed for Ned Granger. But when he returned carrying a paper cup filled with water, he found that the old woman had vanished.

Across town, in the safety of her own living room, Diana stood holding her mother's hand in front of John and Ned Granger.

"Tell us everything, Diana. You don't have to be scared," John said as he put his hands on her shoulders. Then he added, "It's important to tell the truth so we can find Miracle."

Diana felt her heart harden enough to justify lying about a girl who had only wanted to know if her mother was dead or alive.

She told them about the mist in the school yard, about Mrs. Mulligan's collapse.

"But then she forced me to run with her to the dock. She grabbed my shirt, and she threatened—" But she could say no more. Her expression grew dark and her words thick. Diana found her mouth filled with a powdery chalk that made her spit repeatedly.

"Diana? What's wrong?" Patty asked. She kneeled before her daughter and slapped her back as the girl gagged and coughed.

Ned Granger ran for water.

"My God," Patty said.

A tiny rose petal dangled from the corner of Diana's mouth. Patty picked it up and held it out to John, who stared wide-eyed.

Each time Diana tried to speak her lies, another rose petal fell—pink, red, white—until there was a small fragrant mound burying her to the ankles.

Patty held Diana's face and looked into her daughter's terrified eyes. She thought of Milagros's journey alone on the sea. Of the ointment that had snatched Mollie back from death's grip. Nothing seemed impossible now.

"Let the truth fall from your lips, Diana. What do you know about what's happened?"

"It said Rosa," Diana gasped between convulsions.

"What said Rosa?"

"The message in the bottle!"

Patty shut her eyes and held John's hand as Diana told them the truth at last. How she had hidden the bottle and used it to hurt Milagros, how she wanted nothing more in the world than for Milagros to go far away and leave her in peace.

At last the petals ceased.

They placed her in the backseat of Ned Granger's car where she curled into a little ball to sleep.

Then, not daring to look at one another for fear that each had gone mad, they all rushed to the pier.

※ ※ ※

Mrs. Mulligan awoke in her room at the mainland hospital at exactly 8:15 P.M., oxygen tubes in her nostrils and flashing heart monitors behind her head. She was very much alive. Her doctors concluded that she'd had a mild heart attack, the result of climbing stairs and rounding up frightened children in a crisis.

Mrs. Pennington, who had never left the hospital since the afternoon, came into the room.

"Aren't these roses wonderful?" she said, placing the spectacular bouquet gently on the nightstand. She had bought the rugosas at the flower shop in the lobby. She patted her friend's hand. "I've not seen any more beautiful in years. Their color and perfume is magnificent. Thank God that you are well, Mildred."

※ ※ ※

"Did you see that?"

The young carnival worker sat on a crate behind the big tent drinking a root beer and enjoying the early evening breeze that was clearing away the strange fog. It had been a long day of hammering in stakes and sweeping out the pigpens. But as tired as he was, he rushed to the end of the dock to get a better look at the water.

His partner, a white-haired gentleman named Clem, was rubbing the crick in his neck and didn't even open his eyes from exhaustion. He was thinking about the only remaining task: dragging bags of stuffed animal prizes to all the carnival games. They could easily grapple with those in the morning. He was doing a quick inventory of what he would have to collect. Brown moose, purple seals, teddy bears with hearts that squeaked.

"Clem, look in the water. It looks like stingrays," called the young man again. "And they're colored." He was pointing at a large splash of magenta.

The old man closed his eyes and let the perfume of roses fill his nose. *Stingrays? We don't have any of those prizes.*

CHAPTER 35

The Runaway

Because the door was old and the lock rusted by the salt air, it took no time at all to break down the door to Old Woman Pérez's apartment. John entered first, his shoulder aching, followed by Ned Granger, who flipped on the lights and kept his right hand near his gun holster. They had followed a trail of blood up the stairs.

The apartment was empty.

"We are too late," Old Woman Pérez said, staring at the shredded letter on the floor. She noted, too, that the quilt was gone. "*Pobrecita,*" she said quietly. She put her hand to her chest and closed her eyes.

"Mrs. Pérez, are you all right?" Ned Granger asked.

"Yes, of course," she said irritably. "Mr. Winters and I must hurry to the water. Stay here, please, in case she comes back," she added to Officer Granger, who had begun to follow.

Old Woman Pérez hobbled down the steps and headed straight for the pier, where as mysteriously as it had arrived, the mist had begun to recede to the ocean. The mist of regret always hung near tragedy, Old Woman Pérez thought with a shudder. She used her cane to maintain her balance as she put her head down and forced her way into the gusts, past the carnival tents and then down to the narrow stretch of sand.

"Where are we going?" John shouted over the wind.

"Hurry, Mr. Winters!" She marched closer and closer to the water's edge, her eyes scanning the horizon. Would she lose her second chance to love a child and watch her grow? She kept her eyes on the water that glittered once again beneath the sunshine.

"There," she said, pointing her cane. John looked and stopped abruptly. Out in the distance, beneath the red mist, a large patch of water glowed with colors. He could see a tiny boat.

Old Woman Pérez hesitated at the water's edge for only a moment, considering her fears. She had never entered the ocean in all the time she could recall; she had never learned to swim as a child. Anything could be lurking below the surface. She took a deep breath to calm herself. Biting her lips and lifting her skirt, she waded into the water unsteadily.

"Wait! Don't!" John called, grabbing for her elbow to steady her. He followed her warily as she continued her march, eyes fixed on the tiny boat.

Then, he finally saw what impelled her to such foolishness. It was not just a boat. It was the dinghy, Milagros's dinghy that he had moved to the pier slips for safekeeping. And there facing the open sea stood the girl, her hair blowing wildly. Her arms were spread apart like the crossbeam of a mast. Standing on the bottom edge of the quilt, she held the top edge wide. The quilt billowed like a canvas sail.

She was dangerously far out, and John knew they would need help from the fishermen if they were to have any hope of reaching her.

And then something else caught his eye, something so terrifying that it sent a jolt of panic to every part of his body. Out near the dinghy, an enormous splash broke through the water, and a creature's black shadow filled the air. It spanned the sky like a bird before slamming its body inches behind the dinghy.

"I'll get help," he gasped.

But Old Woman Pérez grabbed his arm and would not release him.

"No, Mr. Winters. She must save herself."

CHAPTER 36

Reconciliations

The violent wall of water slammed into the dinghy and drenched Milagros to the skin as she was blown ever closer to the red cloud.

She grabbed the sides for dear life, her heart hardened with purpose. She had spied the rays from the apartment window and knew at once she must face the mist and go to them. It was a sign, she was sure of it. A sign about Rosa.

But now, as the dinghy lurched violently from side to side, Milagros fell to her knees, wondering if she had been tricked. She looked over her shoulder and cowered. A manta, a devil ray, was thrashing dangerously near her. Very clearly, it wanted her out of the boat. It emerged from the water in another terrifying leap. It spread its black wings wide, hovered like a nightmare over her, and crashed down again. Half of her dinghy sank in the ensuing swell, and Milagros scampered to the dry end.

She looked out desperately at the rays shimmering in the deep water, none moving to save her. What was happening here? Were they as afraid as she was?

The manta circled at a dizzying speed and disappeared underwater. Milagros braced herself, white-knuckled, as it jabbed the dinghy roughly with its horned snout, tossing it several feet into the air. Her heart pounded as her mind raced for an answer.

Milagros closed her eyes, trembling. She had seen this enormous creature before. Rosa had said it was harmless despite its size. But how could she explain this angry, agitated creature attacking her now? What if its name was an apt one, after all? What if the wives' tales about devil rays were true?

See with your own eyes, she told herself. *See with your own eyes.*

Again, Milagros spotted the colorful rays. Logic would have told anyone not to believe in them. But she had, and they had cared for her well. What had she to lose by trusting them now, even this gargantuan one before her? She imagined herself on Las Brisas, the great beast taking the shrimp from her palm.

The manta stilled before her, and Milagros opened her eyes and breathed deeply. She struggled carefully to her knees, her eyes still on the manta. With only faith to protect her, she dived toward the blackness.

The chilly clutch of the black manta was unmistakable. It coiled the tip of its massive wing around her like a vise. With one easy motion, the manta sank with Milagros quietly in its grip.

They were moving faster than Milagros could imagine possible, her head cutting through the water like a ship's figurehead prow. They zoomed close to the gritty sand and then—when her lungs seemed about to burst—the manta broke into the air like a bird. Each time, Milagros took a big gulp of air before they dived beneath again.

She should have been afraid, she knew, wrapped helplessly in a devil ray's wing with no idea of her destination.

But she was not. She was afraid of nothing at last. Not of death at the bottom of the sea. Not of gossip or nightmares. Not of Miguel. Not of losing Old Woman Pérez or even of losing everything and everyone she had ever loved on Las Brisas.

There, in the ray's grip, she surrendered her doubt. She accepted the journey—wherever it might take her.

At last, the manta's grasp slackened, and Milagros kicked her sore limbs until she broke the surface. When she emerged, she gasped in delight.

She found herself in the perfect center of the rays, hundreds and hundreds of every type of ray she had ever seen. Their iridescent bodies were pressed tightly to form a wall around her. Only the black manta floated some distance apart.

The scent of roses was so strong now that it stung Milagros's nose. She breathed in deeply, recognizing the scent of Rosa's groves. She knew she would find her. She swam gently among the rays, caressing their backs, looking carefully over each.

And then she saw a single, magnificent ray, shimmering and opalescent like a pink pearl. Milagros stretched her hand into the water and touched the slippery body. It rolled on its back and grazed her hand, gently slurping her arm with its mouth. Then, it fixed its deep black eyes on hers.

Milagros gazed at the ray for a long time, speechless. Slowly, she reached toward the creature and ran her arms over the pink flesh. She closed her eyes. As she had done so many times in her life, Milagros listened for the truth. Could it be? Was this possible? She let her face linger against the cool skin, trying to remember all she could of her mother's face.

Without warning, she saw it clearly, a pearl tucked inside a tiny fold of her memory. Not the terrified face of their last moment on Las Brisas, but a long-ago forgotten day. Milagros could almost feel the damp ground in the groves, hear the sound of her own giggling as she waited for her mother to discover her and give chase along the shady rows. Rosa's hair shiny in the mottled sun, her normally tight-lipped smile breaking into a wide grin: "There you are!"

How old had she been? Milagros could not remember. It had been so long ago that they had played together. But the memory was so clear she could feel it. When she opened her eyes, she was smiling. She knew at last what was true. She kissed the ray's pink skin lightly.

"Mamá."

I have found you, whispered Rosa, her voice now part of the ocean's lull.

Milagros smiled. "And I you."

Rosa encircled her child in her powerful wings. Then she rolled them both over in the water. Breaking the surface, Milagros let out a small laugh of relief. They took turns doing somersaults beneath the surface and blowing bubbles of water. They raced to the sandy bottom and back. They found pleasure in nothing more than each other's idle company. And in their innocent games, they each chased every suspicion and regret far from their hearts, sending them all into the sea, where they best lived in the bellies of hungry sharks.

Breathless at last, Milagros floated on her back with

her eyes scanning the boundless sky. It would be so lovely, she thought, to stay here in the ocean with Rosa, to join all these spectacular creatures. Together they would find broken people scattered at the edge of every sea and help them see magic with their own eyes, protect them from any harm.

But too soon, Rosa interrupted her thoughts: *Get on,* she signaled, lowering herself beneath the surface.

Milagros climbed onto her mother's back, propping her chin and spreading her arms wide over her mother's wings. The rays opened their circle at the closest point to the shore. Rosa headed inland.

Between their shallow dives, Milagros could see bits of her life in Holly Pointe. The pier was now lined with carnival workers and other stunned onlookers who pointed and shouted at the light emanating from the water. But only one person mattered to Milagros. There, standing alone in the shallow water, was Old Woman Pérez. Her friend had not abandoned her after all. Milagros slid off Rosa and swam toward her quickly.

"Do not be afraid, *señora.* It is safe," she called to Old Woman Pérez as they approached. She took her hand and rested the other along Rosa's spine. "I have found her, *señora.* It is my mother, Rosa."

Old Woman Pérez looked dubiously at the ray before her. Could such a thing be true?

"Close your eyes," Milagros said, placing her palms over her friend's face. "Listen. She will tell you."

They felt the water grow warm and scented. Soon police sirens grew distant, and they could hear only the gentle splash of Rosa's body as she glided through their legs. Fear melted away. In its place was a welcome happiness she had long ago forgotten: the unperturbed peace of holding one's sleeping child under the moonlight. *Yes,* she told herself. *This was the girl's true mamá.*

She opened her eyes and regarded the ray. *You have raised a strong girl, Rosa Santiago de la Torre. A strong girl born of a strong woman before her.*

Rosa bowed her snout slightly.

Milagros interrupted them with a gasp, remembering the dinghy. "Wait! Come, Mamá, hurry." She climbed onto Rosa's back once again and pointed to the tip of her dinghy still floating in the sea.

When they returned, Milagros held the quilt. She spread it open, handing Old Woman Pérez one end. Rosa grazed her graceful disk over the colors.

It is a lovely manta, she told them with a splash.

Milagros and Old Woman Pérez beamed. *And so, might I add, are you, Señora Rosa,* Old Woman Pérez said.

Glancing up at the setting sun, Rosa circled Milagros one last time. She hovered and held her daughter in her gaze.

It is time for me to go.

"Please, a while longer, Mamá," Milagros begged. "Don't leave me yet."

But Rosa swam just out of her reach.

I must go, Milagros. But I do not leave you. My mark is on you and yours on me. It is the way of mothers and daughters through all time.

And with that, Rosa turned toward the sea. *You will be well together.*

CHAPTER 37

A New Beginning

All that summer, Holly Pointe buzzed with excitement. The summer festival opened, John's *pastel* was a sensation, and to the delight of the festival organizers, the rays lingered in the bay for the entire duration, a spectacle that lured Away crowds who were welcomed for the first time to Holly Pointe. It would become an annual occurrence called Miracle's Rays, one that, along with an unusually large and early explosion of rugosa blooms, delighted the children of Holly Pointe each year. And none was more delighted, of course, than Milagros, who knew it was Rosa reminding her she was loved.

Milagros and Old Woman Pérez hung their first-prize quilt on the front door of the apartment as a testament to their friendship. Milagros soon moved in permanently, with John and Patty's blessing. She and Old Woman Pérez would live many years together, joined in the summer months by Mercedes and Héctor, who grew to love Milagros as one of their own.

It was only when Old Woman Pérez could no longer climb the wobbly steps that they eventually moved to a small cottage. It was not far from the Winterses' home or from the tailor-and-mend shop, where they could still keep a view of the bay. The Pérez/De la Torre house— where the windows were often open and the garden exploded with all manner of fruits and vegetables—was the only home in all of Holly Pointe painted lovingly with the guidance of Patty Winters. It was a bright purple and orange.

Years later, long after she had forgiven any harm that had come to her, Milagros would say she had lived two lives as two girls. The first life in Las Brisas, a paradise where much sorrow began. And the second in Holly Pointe, a town that felt sterile and cold, but where she learned that, like wildflowers in the granite cliffs, happiness could take root in the most unlikely places. In the end, it was not the place that made any difference to a girl's happiness at all.

It was as Rosa had said when they first met the rays. To find joy and magic in life you must look inside yourself and see beyond what others see. *See yourself with your own eyes.* This was the message that Milagros finally sealed in her own bottle and dropped into the bay with Héctor at her side. Together they stood on the pier and blew the bottle toward the ocean for good luck. The current pulled it away slowly, first in the direction of the Winterses' home, and then out to sea. Perhaps, Milagros told him, their bottle would travel the whole world before it found just the right shore. But it would find its way to the right hands eventually. Such bottles always did. And waiting there would be a lonely child, a worried mother, or even the sad ghost of a pirate seeking forgiveness.

Acknowledgments

I am grateful to so many people who helped me bring *Milagros* to life. My agent, Jennifer Jaeger, has been a champion of this novel from the start, and I thank her for the enthusiasm and energy she brought to finding it a good home. I offer huge thanks also to my extraordinary editor, Christy Ottaviano, and the fine editorial and art team at Henry Holt Books for Young Readers. They helped me make this novel much stronger than I could have ever done alone. *¡Mil gracias a todos!*

Along the way, I relied heavily on friends who agreed to read early manuscripts and offer advice. Among the many helping hands were a few that proved indispensable. *Un abrazo fuerte para:* Liz Whitehurst for the many quiet conversations we had about our projects; Lucinda Whitehurst, editor of *The Open Book* newsletter and librarian at St. Christopher's Lower School in Richmond,

Virginia, for being a good set of "professional eyes"; Sandra Peterson, a proud and true Mainer, for giving me what I needed to reshape Holly Pointe; Jennifer Palazzolo for her Web design; Laura Rugless for her clever ideas and thoughtful reading; Alice Fitzgerald for her unyielding belief that I could do it; and Ann Foster for giving me hope, enthusiasm, and grit when I couldn't muster them myself.

Thanks are also due to the members of the Mother Daughter Book Club: Sandra Menéndez; Jennifer and Sarah Palazzolo; Debbie and Becky Seidel; Sheldon and Haley Maguire; Nancy and Anne Hamner; Lynn and Caroline Medley; Sarah Woodhouse and Amanda Orchowsky; and Kaye and Molly Gardner. Their book choices and intelligent discussions reconnected me to writing for young people. *Gracias, chicas,* for inspiring me to reach for a story worthy of your thinking.

To Raquel Jaramillo, whose art graces the jacket of this novel, I can only offer what we both shared as childhood best friends: devotion, the hope for endless adventures, and love. Destiny carved out our unexpected reunion as adults, and working with her has been an honor. *¿Quién nos iba decir?*

Finally, I offer thanks and love to my entire family for their support. This is especially true of my husband,

ACKNOWLEDGMENTS

Javier Menéndez, and our three children, Cristina, Sandra, and Alex. They waited patiently as I spent months wandering in the imaginary lands of Las Brisas and Holly Pointe. They are *my* Home and the brightest light I have ever known. *Los quiero a todos mucho.*